The
Great Race
to
Sycamore
Street

J. Samia Mair

KUBE PUBLISHING
CHILDREN'S BOOKS

The Great Race to Sycamore Street

Published by
KUBE PUBLISHING LTD.,
MCC, Ratby Lane, Markfield, Leicestershire, LE67 9SY, UK.
Tel +44 (01530) 249230, Fax +44 (01530) 249656
E-mail: info@kubepublishing.com
Website: www.kubepublishing.com

Please note that US English has been used throughout
this book.

Author J. Samia Mair
Illustrator James Cottell
Book design Nasir Cadir
Editor Yosef Smyth

Printed by Imak Ofset, Turkey

A Cataloguing-in-Publication Data record for this book is
available from the British Library

ISBN 978-1-84774-057-1

*I dedicate this book to my daughters,
Mei-Ying and Mei-Lin, who inspire my writing
and bring much joy to my life.*

Cicada Surprise

HUDE had seconds to decide. The other motorcycles were closing in fast. He could ride down a steep mountain pass leading to who-knows-where. Or, he could follow the train tracks into a mysterious tunnel. Either way, he was taking a big chance.

Hude grabbed the throttle and pulled a wheelie. He headed straight into the dark hole. A strange tingling feeling flowed from the handlebars through his hands, arms and shoulders. He checked the speedometer. He had reached the seventy miles-per-hour mark. That wasn't fast enough. He had to go faster if he wanted to escape.

Suddenly, an eerie golden glow raced towards him. It was a train! He had to get out of the tunnel and now.

Swish. The speeding train passed by him just as he exited. The wind almost knocked him down.

Too close, Hude thought to himself.

He was now riding on a narrow road, twisting down the side of a mountain. His bike was nearly horizontal through the curves. Showers of sparks flew up from the pavement.

"Rainbows!" Hude yelled when he saw puddles of oil in front of him.

He could not avoid them all, and his bike slid out of control. When he swerved to avoid a tree, he came dangerously close to falling off a cliff. Somehow he managed to get back on the road. But his troubles were not over.

A truck ahead of him blew a tire. Pieces of shredded tire littered the road. He weaved in and out, not daring to slow down.

Out of nowhere, the motorcycles chasing him appeared. He looked ahead. He was coming to a bridge. A section in the middle was missing! But he had no choice. He had to go for it. The other motorcycles screeched to a stop. Hude rolled the throttle. He lowered his head and torso close to the bike. The motorcycle soared into the air.

"Come on, come on, come on! ... Bummer. I bit it!"

"What happened?" Amani asked Hude, her ten-year-old brother.

They were sitting across from each other in a train, heading towards their grandmother's house in the country.

"I leveled up in my new game *Xtreme Motorcycle Meat Grinder II*. I was riding a Busa Ninja X1000. If I had captured the nitrous, I could have injected it into my engine. It would have given me an instant power boost to clear the bridge."

Amani peeked behind her, not sure where the three boys had gone. They had been causing trouble on the train ever since Baltimore. All she wanted to do was to read and write in her journal. But instead she was worrying about flying paper airplanes, tossed peanuts and spitballs.

"Do you see them anywhere?" Amani asked, but Hude did not answer.

"Hude, Hude, Hude!" Amani said loudly. "Will you stop playing that thing for a minute and listen to me?"

"What did you say?" Hude said without looking up.

"I asked you if you knew where those boys went. I don't see them. It makes me more nervous not knowing where they are than having them around. I just know they're up to no good."

Hude looked up from his game and scanned the train compartment with his eyes.

"Maybe they got off at the last stop. Just ignore them if they come back. We'll be at Grandma's soon anyway. You'll never have to see them again."

Amani looked around. Maybe Hude was right. The troublesome boys were nowhere to be seen. She opened her book and resumed reading.

Amani wasn't your typical nine-year-old girl. She wasn't into fashion or celebrities or the latest school gossip. She liked books, especially adventure stories that took her to exciting places and put her in the middle of tricky situations. Everyone knew she was a bookworm. She even looked like a bookworm. She had short bangs that fell straight on her forehead. The rest of her hair was always in two braids that hung above her shoulders. She wore small, round, wire-rimmed glasses that appeared even more round against her heart-shaped face. She dressed in four colors only: tan, green, blue and orange. Colors that she imagined her adventure heroes would wear—sensible with a little flash, as she described it. And she never went anywhere without her small backpack that she got at the zoo. Inside it was everything an aspiring author would need—books, journal, sharpened pencils, assorted color pens and, of course, a muse, something that inspired her writing. No respectable author would be caught without one. Her latest muse was a stuffed animal panda bear that she named Mr. Panda. Her mother had given it to her at the 30th Street Train Station in Philadelphia before they left.

Hude, on the other hand, was a typical tweenaged boy. He loved any and all things electronic. If it were up to him, he would spend most of his time playing on his Wii, behind his computer, or with his Sony PSP. But it wasn't up to him, as his parents would often remind him. Fortunately, he liked to play sports as well. Ice hockey had always been his favorite sport and living in Philadelphia, he was a big Flyers fan. But now he spent a lot of time shooting arrows. His grandfather had first taught him to shoot with toy arrows that had a rubber suction cup as a tip. Now he was regularly participating in competitions. Hanging on his wall was his grandfather's recurve composite bow, waiting for him to grow into.

While Amani was thrilled to be visiting their grandmother in the country for a few weeks, Hude would have preferred that his grandmother visit them in Philadelphia. He had everything that he needed in the city. The slow pace of country life bored him. And his parents had told him no video games at his grandmother's house. He didn't know how he was going to survive. At least he had entered a target archery competition at the County Fair. The top two winners took home prize money, and there were some new video games that he really wanted to buy.

"They're back," Amani whispered to her brother.

Hude didn't hear her. Amani looked at the boys out of the corner of her eye. The three boys sat down two seats behind them and across the aisle. They had never sat so close before and they were looking at something in a white Styrofoam cup.

"Hey, Bobby. Give me that!" a boy said as he tried to grab the cup.

"Just wait a second," Bobby told him.

Then the unthinkable happened. Bobby got up and passed by Amani. Before she knew what was happening, he dumped something from the Styrofoam cup on top of her open book.

"AHHHHHH!" Amani screamed.

She jumped up. She threw the book towards Hude and ran away down the aisle.

"What is that?" Hude said to no one in particular.

A huge black beetle-like bug with two enormous beady red eyes sat on the seat next to him. Orange veins ran through its clear wings. He had never seen anything like it before. He then noticed the boys laughing hysterically. He looked around. No sign of Amani. It wasn't hard for him to put the pieces together.

"Next stop, Fairfax County," a voice announced over the intercom.

It was their stop. As the enormous beady eyes stared at him, Hude thought it was probably a good time to get up anyway. He collected their belongings, including Amani's backpack which she had left on the seat. He found her book on the floor and laughed when he read the title, *Lost in the Amazon: The Daring Adventures of Tad Walker*.

Must be a lot of bugs like this one down there, he thought.

The boys were now sitting quietly in their seats. It wasn't until he walked past them that he realized why. Across from them sat a man with a stern look on his face. He was wearing a dark blue uniform with red stitching and a gold patch. On top of his head was a matching blue cap with a black, shiny, stiff bill and gold trim.

He was the man who had collected their tickets in Philadelphia.

I guess those boys are his problem now, Hude thought, as he walked into the next train compartment.

Before leaving, though, he noticed that one of the boys was wearing a white T-shirt with a picture of a blue bow strung with a blue arrow with red fletching. The word JOAD was written in big red letters across it. Hude knew that JOAD (pronounced JOE-ADD) stood for Junior Olympic Archery Development. Only serious archers belonged to that group. Although Hude didn't know it, the boy noticed him too. Bobby McPherson noticed the bow case that Hude was carrying.

The train slowed down to stop. Hude found Amani standing by the door in the next compartment. He handed her backpack and book to her.

"I can't wait to get some peace and quiet in the country," she said.

Hude thought Amani might cry when they stepped outside onto the train platform. Millions of those large black beetle-like bugs darted jerkily in the air. They hovered together near the trees, looking like small black clouds. People in the parking lot dashed to their cars for cover.

"What is happening here?" Amani asked in a panicked tone.

"Don't you worry about those little things, honey. They won't hurt you," a familiar voice said from behind them.

Amani and Hude turned around. "Grandma!"

They both hugged her at the same time.

"I can't believe how much you have grown. Hude, you are almost as tall as me! And Amani, you look just like your mother when she was your age. Seeing you on Skype certainly isn't the same as in person."

"You haven't changed a bit, Grandma," Amani said. "And that's just the way I like it."

Grandma Hana was a petite woman with a big heart. She was wearing an Amish straw hat from Lancaster over a scarf made in Turkey. Her long, pale green cotton Pakistani kameez fit comfortably over her American-made pants. She had leather Moroccan sandals on her feet and a handmade bag made of Yemeni cloth across one shoulder. She, like the country of her birth, was a mixture of cultures that somehow seemed to work.

No one had ever heard Grandma Hana say a mean thing about anyone. If something good happened to her, she said *"alhamdulillah."* If something bad happened to her, she said "alhamdulillah." Her whole being sparkled like her blue eyes. Just being around her made you feel good.

"I want to hear all about your first train ride by yourselves," Grandma Hana said. "We have so much to catch up on. For one thing, a new family is moving in behind us. And I can't wait for you to see the farmhouse. It looks just as it did when I left. And the peach tree. I think it's going to be a great harvest this year, *inshallah.*"

Grandma Hana had spent the last two years in Turkey. She had met and married their grandfather in Istanbul over forty years ago. They both converted in the Blue Mosque. After he died two years ago, she decided to return for a visit. A few weeks turned into a few months, and months turned into years. She had rented out the farmhouse while she was away. Her old friends Fenby Moore and his wife, Hazel, took care of everything that needed to be done at home. This was the first time Hude and Amani had seen their grandmother since she had returned to the United States.

"What *are* these horrible things, Grandma?" Amani asked as she jumped out of the way of an incoming bug.

"They're seventeen-year cicadas. They live in the ground and feed on tree roots. After seventeen years, they crawl out to mate. The males make those sounds to attract the females. After mating, the males die. The female cuts tiny slits in small tree branches where she deposits eggs. After she lays her eggs, she dies. The eggs hatch and the nymphs fall to the ground and dig about twelve inches under. Seventeen years later, they crawl out of the ground and the cycle starts again."

"They're disgusting," Amani commented.

"But harmless," Grandma Hana smiled. "They don't bite, sting or chew. They're terrible flyers, so you can outrun them. Although I did get one caught in my hijab seventeen years ago and that wasn't particularly pleasant."

Amani shivered at the thought. Grandma Hana continued.

"They survive because of their numbers. There are so many bugs that predators can't possibly eat them all. Everything likes to eat them—dogs, cats, birds, squirrels, deer, raccoons, mice, ants, wasps and even humans."

"Humans!" Amani shrieked.

"Let me show you," Grandma Hana pointed to a food cart in the parking lot. "I'm parked right near it."

Amani, Hude and their grandmother walked towards her car. A crowd was standing around the food cart. To Amani's horror people were waiting in line to order. The menu was listed on a large, handwritten poster board: "Roasted Cicada, Cicada Stir-Fry, Soft-Shelled Cicada, Chocolate-Covered Cicada, Cicada Surprise…." Amani stopped reading at Cicada Surprise. She started feeling sick.

"Tasty, yum!" someone yelled from the crowd.

Amani and Hude looked over. A boy was crunching on a mouthful of roasted cicadas. He held several others in his hand. When the boy saw Amani and Hude he started to laugh. Bits of half-chewed cicada fell out of his mouth and onto his T-shirt. Hude recognized the boy and the T-shirt immediately. Amani also recognized the boy, Bobby, from the train. This was the first time that she had gotten a good look at him. It was difficult to determine the exact color of Bobby's hair because it was buzzed so closely to his head. He was shorter than her brother but around his age. He was wearing a red, white, and blue T-shirt that said JOAD on it. Amani had seen that word before when she went with Hude to target practice.

Looking at Bobby, Amani somehow knew that her summer vacation in the country wasn't going to be quiet and peaceful. And Hude believed that he would see that boy again. They were both right.

The peach tree
on Sycamore Street

GRANDMA Hana lived on Sycamore Street in the small town of Cherry Hill in Fairfax County, Maryland. The funny thing about it was that there were no sycamore trees on Sycamore Street and, as far as anyone knew, no hill anywhere in town covered with cherries. But there was Grandma Hana's famous peach tree.

The peach tree first became famous because Grandma Hana had planted a nectarine pit. She had eaten a freshly picked nectarine that was so delicious that she decided to plant the pit. But instead of growing a nectarine tree, the pit turned into a peach tree. As she later learned, peaches and nectarines are so closely related that sometimes when you plant one, you get the other. The second thing that made the tree famous was the way the peaches tasted. The honey-colored flesh was smooth and oozed with juice. Each bite had the perfect mixture of sweetness and tanginess. Grandma Hana's peaches tasted like peaches should taste, and like no other peaches in all of Maryland. The third reason for the tree's fame was its strength. It had survived ice storms, blizzards, hurricanes, and all sorts of pests and diseases that took down countless other trees. Yet it never failed to produce the best peaches, even though it was more than thirty years old, decades past what should have been its peak. What made the tree the most famous of all was that Grandma Hana's peach pie never lost the pie contest at the Fairfax County Fair. Friends, neighbors, just about anyone who knew about the peach tree, looked forward to the harvest, so they could eat some of Grandma Hana's pie. At one point, a businessman approached Grandma Hana and offered to help her start a business selling pies. But Grandma turned the offer down. She told him that "peaches were a gift from God and gifts were meant to be shared."

Splat!

A huge cicada smashed loudly against the front windshield of their grandmother's car and stuck there.

"Ahhh!" Hude yelled like a young girl and jumped back in his seat.

He was sitting in the front passenger's seat but it was still hard for Amani to hear him amongst the deafening, screeching, shrill sound of the cicadas.

"This is awesome!" Hude yelled, smiling back at Amani.

This unwelcome bug adventure was decidedly not awesome, Amani thought.

It was one thing reading about Tad Walker and the ginormous Hercules beetle he discovered in his hammock. It was quite another thing to experience a ginormous bug oneself!

"When will this end, Grandma?" Hana yelled up front.

"It's been going on for a few weeks now. In a few days we'll be back to the normal sounds of summer." Grandma Hanna smiled. "You'll be twenty-six years old before you see this glorious show again, inshallah."

"Too soon as far as I'm concerned," Amani said.

Trying to forget the world around her, Amani imagined the delicious smell of peaches ripening on the tree. Nothing compared to biting into a freshly picked, perfectly ripe peach on a hot summer day. The first bite of the season was always the best. When she was younger, she looked forward to the peach harvest every year. Until that moment, she hadn't realized how much she had missed the last couple of summers with her grandmother. She thought she had outgrown some things like the rope swing and playing hide-and-seek in the cornfield next to her grandmother's house. Amani breathed in deeply. The smell of horse manure seeped through the car windows. Her thoughts were flooded with childhood memories.

Grandma Hana stopped the car in front of 494 Sycamore Street. Everything looked the same—except, of course, for the swarms of cicadas in the air. The old white farmhouse sat on a large tract of green grass. Multicolored echinacea, climbing roses, gerbera daisies, and many other flowers that Amani could not name were in full bloom everywhere.

Grandma's house always looks as if a rainbow has fallen from the sky and painted it, Amani thought.

She liked the way that sounded and made a mental note to write the sentence down in her journal when she got inside.

The front porch wrapped around one side of the house. Two weather-worn rocking chairs and a large gliding chair sat in their same spots on the porch. She and her brother had spent many summer evenings there, listening to their grandfather's stories, while their grandmother crocheted delicate lacework for her scarves. Looking at the porch, Amani could almost smell her grandfather's musk perfume. It was the only perfume that he used. He told her that the Prophet Muhammad, peace be upon him, said that musk was the most fragrant of scents and that the sweat of people in paradise smelled like musk. Her grandfather's eyes would tear when he said that the Prophet's scent was described as more fragrant than musk.

But the heart of the farmhouse was the extraordinarily large peach tree in the backyard. It was planted in the center of a small rise at the end of their grandmother's property that sloped down to the neighbor's property. It stood majestically, like a priceless sculpture displayed in a museum. Each season brought new beauty. In spring, clusters of pink blossoms erupted as one. In autumn, slender leaves drifted to the earth, encircling the tree in a carpet of coppery brown. In winter, snow rested on the branches outlining the tree in sparkling white. But nothing compared to summer, when the tree burst with glistening golden-orange fruit, surrounded by bright green leaves against a vast blue sky.

To the right of the farmhouse was a cornfield. Woods were to the left. Although it was overgrown, Amani could still see the entrance to the path that led to the lake with the rope swing.

"That's weird, Grandma," Hude said. "The cicadas seem to be attacking only the trees with leaves. The pine trees don't seem to be bothered at all."

"Grandma, the peach tree!" Amani yelled.

Grandma Hana turned around.

"Don't worry, dear. The peach tree is fine, alhamdulillah. Mr. Fenby helped me cover it with netting."

Grandma Hana noticed Hude's bow case on the seat next to Amani.

"Hude, I have a surprise for you inside. It's something Grandpop would have wanted you to have."

Hude jumped out of the car first and grabbed his belongings. Amani followed, holding her suitcase in one hand and shielding her face with her backpack in the other. They zigzagged to the front door, dodging bugs. Hude stopped briefly and a cicada landed on his shirt. Feeling brave, he picked it up. But the bug buzzed so loudly he dropped it almost immediately. Amani didn't stop running until she was inside.

The new neighbors

A FEW days had gone by. Hude had spent most of his time in his grandfather's workshop in the basement with the surprise Grandma Hana had given him. It was his grandfather's archery notebook.

It was filled with all sorts of useful advice about how to shoot better. Hude realized that he had been making some mistakes. His grandfather had also written step-by-step instructions on how to build a superior bow and what arrows worked best in different conditions. Hude was more excited than ever about the archery competition.

Amani spent *all* of her time inside. She wanted nothing more to do with the seventeen-year cicadas. She had finished the Tad Walker adventure in the Amazon and was now reading the next book in the series. This time Tad Walker was in a race against his arch-enemy, who wanted to destroy a priceless aboriginal totem pole. Just as she got to the part where the hero was jumping out of a plane into an uncharted jungle, Hude burst into the room where she was reading.

"It's safe to go outside now!" he exclaimed. "You won't believe how cool it is out there."

Amani looked out of the window. Not a single cicada in the air. The invasion was over. It was safe to go outside. Safe, if you didn't mind walking on a carpet of cicada carcasses. A neighbor's orange tabby cat named Miss Ginger lay lazily on the front walkway, passing a dying cicada back and forth between her front paws. Hude was on the front lawn picking up dead bugs. He had almost filled an entire trash bag. He was enjoying himself so much that as soon as he finished Grandma Hana's lawn, he picked up all of the cicadas on the new neighbors' property. He then offered to help an older couple down the street clean their yard. Hude asked Amani if she wanted to help, but she declined. She was writing all about it in her journal.

"I smell chocolate chip cookies!" Hude said excitedly when he returned about an hour later.

He reached for a cookie on the kitchen table, but Amani pushed his hand away.

"These are for the new neighbors," Amani told him. "Ours are still baking in the oven."

"Does it make a difference? I mean, they're all from the same dough, aren't they? I can eat one of these cookies now and replace it with one of ours when they're done."

Hude again reached for a cookie and again Amani pushed his hand away.

"It does make a difference, Hude. I made sure that all of the cookies in this batch are the same size and perfectly round. I also put extra chocolate chips in them. We want to make a good first impression, don't we?"

"I guarantee you that the new neighbors will not know the difference," Hude said.

"But I will," Amani said in a tone that meant she wasn't going to budge.

There were two things that his sister took seriously—writing and baking. When she had her mind made up about one of them, it was no use trying to persuade her otherwise.

"Where's Grandma?" Hude asked, changing the subject.

"She's in the garden. I'm sure she could use your help."

Hude quickly gulped down a glass of water before leaving through the kitchen door that led to the back patio.

"Here, let me do that Grandma," he said.

Hude helped Grandma Hana move a large bag of mushroom manure across the lawn to her vegetable garden. He opened the bag and dumped it next to the pumpkin plants.

A few minutes later Fenby Moore pulled up his old, long bed pickup truck in front of the new neighbors' house. The truck was dark green with the words 'Fenby Moore's Landscaping and Yard Service' painted in yellow on the side doors. Hanging from the rear-view mirror was a faded macramé bracelet that his only daughter had made him decades ago. Mr. Fenby was like his truck—dependable, straightforward, loyal and sentimental. He was dressed in a brown plaid button-down shirt with the sleeves rolled up just above his elbows. His blue jeans were nearly white, worn in through years of wear. He wore a dark gray baseball cap with the name of a local hardware store stitched in black on the front. His work boots were old but comfortable. He wasn't tall, but he was strong, especially for a man his age. His skin was tan, rough, and he had hard calluses on his palms. He didn't speak a lot but always had a kind word to say.

Fenby Moore grabbed some equipment from the bed of his truck. He pulled out a piece of paper from the pocket of his shirt and studied it for a while. He made some measurements and then started to put stakes in the ground around the perimeter of the neighbors' property. As he approached the peach tree, he stopped. He then noticed Hana and her grandson in the garden. He walked over to say hello.

"Could that be Hude? Last time I saw you, you were only this high," he said, putting his hand out in the air about waist high.

"It is indeed. I couldn't believe it myself," Grandma Hana said. "Wait until you see Amani. She looks just like Sarah."

At that precise moment Amani walked outside holding two plates of chocolate chip cookies.

"Mr. Fenby, I didn't know you were here!" Amani said.

She quickly set the cookies on the patio table and ran over to see him. Mr. Fenby had always been one of her favorite people.

"My, my, young lady. It's true. You do look just like your mother."

Amani blushed at the comment. She thought her mother was beautiful.

"Are your parents visiting too?" Mr. Fenby asked.

"No, they stayed in Philadelphia. But they'll be coming to pick us up in a couple of weeks, after the County Fair."

"You know I'm counting down the days to the Fair," Mr. Fenby said. "I can't wait to have some of your grandmother's peach pie. The County Fair hasn't been the same without it, the last two years."

"You mean my grandmother's and my peach pie," Amani said proudly. "We're entering the contest together."

"Then, I bet it will be the best peach pie ever," Mr. Fenby said.

Amani smiled.

"I see that the peaches are starting to break color, Hana. When do you expect to harvest?" Mr. Fenby asked.

"God decides that," Grandma Hana said, "but I'm guessing about a week, inshallah. Harvest is near. And this year Hude is entered in the archery competition. He has been studying Garrett's old notes."

"The fruit doesn't fall far from the tree, " Mr. Fenby said. "Hude, you probably know this, but your grandfather was the state champion. He made us all proud. There hasn't been an archer like your grandfather in Fairfax County since he competed. There is this thirteen-year-old boy, J.J. McPherson, who is showing some talent. The one to watch, though, is his younger brother Bobby. He's about your age. Keep an eye on those brothers. They will be your stiffest competition."

"I will Mr. Fenby," Hude said.

"Well, I better be getting back to work. Mr. Carr is moving in today. He wanted me to get a few things started before his wife and son join him. Which reminds me, Mr. Carr wants to put a fence around his property. According to the surveyor's report, your peach tree is about a foot over the property line. Do you think that could be accurate?"

"I don't know," Grandma Hana said. "We planted that tree so long ago, long before the lots on that side of the neighborhood were measured out."

"Well, it shouldn't matter. I'm sure Mr. Carr won't mind putting the fence back a bit."

"Look, the moving truck is here," Amani said.

A large moving van slowed down in front of Mr. Carr's house and parked out of sight.

"I better be going then. Mr. Carr is probably right behind. But I think I'll grab one of those delicious smelling cookies before I do," Mr. Fenby said.

"Help yourself, Mr. Fenby," Amani said. "Take some from the pretty plate. The cookies on the other plate are still cooling."

"I think that I'll grab one of those delicious smelling cookies as well," Hude said.

"Nice try," Amani replied, giving him her look. "Grandma, you don't think the fence is going to be a problem with the peach tree, do you?"

"I shouldn't think so. It's easy enough to work around the tree. It's a shame though. The fence will block his view. What is more beautiful than a peach tree ready for harvest? *Subhanallah.*"

"But what...what if Mr. Carr doesn't want to do that?" Amani asked. "What if he wants his fence where the tree is? You don't think he would cut down the tree, do you?"

"Of course not, dear," Grandma Hana said. "What kind of person would cut down a tree like that?"

The sound of screeching tires interrupted their conversation. An expensive black SUV pulled up behind the moving van. It stopped so abruptly, the vehicle bounced. The driver's door opened and a man in a dark gray suit stepped out. As soon as he opened the back door of the car, a yellow Labrador retriever burst out, like a rocket taking off. The dog ran all around the neighbor's yard, frantically sniffing at some dead cicadas that Hude had missed and barking loudly. The dog stopped momentarily as Mr. Fenby approached, smelling the piece of cookie in his hand. The dog lunged for it, but Mr. Fenby plopped the cookie in his mouth before the dog could get it. Mr. Carr reached into the SUV and pulled out his briefcase. He looked back and saw his dog and Mr. Fenby. Without saying a word to either of them, he turned around and walked toward his house. The dog went back to sniffing the air. Mr. Fenby decided that it was a good time to leave. He would talk to Mr. Carr another time.

The dog looked over at Grandma Hana's property. Without warning, he started running towards them at full speed. He trampled several of Grandma Hana's daylilies and uprooted others. Hude ran to stop the dog but he wasn't quick enough. The dog rushed past Hude, nearly knocking him over. The dog jumped the rabbit fence around the vegetable garden and chomped on a large, red tomato the size of a tennis ball. Juice squirted all over Grandma Hana and Amani, who were trying to grab his collar. By this time, Hude was at the vegetable garden. He lunged at the dog but missed, landing in the pile of mushroom manure. Attracted by the scent of rosemary, the dog sniffed his way over to the herb section, skewering several yellow squash with his toenails on the way. The lavender and basil made him sneeze. Hot slobber sprayed everywhere. Unsatisfied, the dog sniffed the air wildly. He still had not found his prize.

"The cookies!" Hude screamed, but it was too late.

The dog darted to the patio and leaped in the air, pushing the patio table on its side. Cookies flew in every direction. The dog scampered around the patio floor, gobbling up everything in his path.

Amani rushed to the patio. The dog was licking up the last crumbs.

"Are they all gone?" Hude asked when he got there.

The dog looked at him, urinated on the lilac bush, and plopped on the grass near where Hude was standing.

"I guess that answers my question, doesn't it."

"Why don't you both bring the dog back to its owner," Grandma Hana said. "I'll start cleaning up this mess."

Hude reached for the dog's collar and noticed a nametag.

"Pal. The dog's name is Pal," he said.

As soon as the dog heard his name, he started to wag his tail.

"They should have named him Trouble," Amani said. "Let's bring him back quickly. I'm in no mood to make a new friend now, especially a four-footed one that eats my cookies."

Hude and Amani started walking toward the new neighbors' house and Pal followed them. As they approached the house, Mr. Carr opened the back door. Pal ran inside. Mr. Carr looked at the two kids in his backyard. They were filthy. Their hair was a mess. Their clothes were disheveled. He did not like what he saw.

"I don't know who you are or what you want, but you should know that I am a very private person. I'd appreciate it if you could respect my privacy and stay off of my property. Have I made myself clear?"

Mr. Carr didn't wait for an answer. He turned around and slammed the door behind him. Hude looked at Amani.

"Is that the kind of first impression you hoped we would make?"

Amani looked back at Hude.

"Is that the kind of person who would cut down a tree?"

What can a peach tree teach you?

Hude and Amani woke up early the next morning to do *Fajr* prayers with their grandmother. Normally they would go back to sleep right afterwards. But today they stayed up to fix the damage that the dog had caused the day before. Amani blamed one person—Mr. Carr. Maybe if he wasn't so mean, his dog would be better behaved. Maybe if he wasn't so mean, she wouldn't have to worry about the peach tree being cut down. The more she thought about it, the angrier she became. Grandma Hana told her last night that the Prophet, peace be upon him, said that it is best to be slow to anger and quick to calm. Amani was trying not to be angry, but she was struggling with it.

Hude wasn't very happy either. But it was not because of Mr. Carr or the dog. In fact, he decided that he liked Pal. If he were a dog, he would have gobbled up those cookies too. His complaint was that the next-gen PlayStation was being released today and he had no way to check it out. His friends in Philadelphia were probably in a long line now, waiting for the store to open. And he hadn't played any video games since he arrived.

"Anyone want some fresh mint iced tea? I think the mint was the only herb the dog didn't uproot," Grandma Hana said cheerfully.

She was the only person living in the white farmhouse on Sycamore Street who was in a good mood.

"Come," Grandma said, noticing that something was wrong. "Let's sit under the peach tree. It has plenty of shade."

"The peaches are so big already, Grandma. It should be a good harvest," Amani said, as they walked to the tree. She was already in a better mood.

"Inshallah," Grandma Hana said. "The blossoms bloomed early. And there was a late freeze. I thought we might lose the entire crop. But alhamdulillah, the peach tree survived another challenge. And did you notice the shape? There's just the right amount of blue between the branches. A peach tree should look like a goblet, with its branches reaching upward and gently angled outward from the trunk. Sunlight and air need to reach every branch. You know where to prune by looking at the blue sky between the branches. It's the empty space that shows you the shape of the tree and not the tree itself. Almost everything can be learned from its opposite. How would you know if you were happy, if you didn't feel sorrow from time to time?"

Amani smiled at Hude. Grandma Hana always knew the right thing to say at the right time. They sat under the peach tree, sipping cold iced tea.

"Why do you think Mr. Carr is so mean, Grandma?" Amani asked, looking at the new neighbors' house.

"Amani." Grandma paused, smiling. "Do you have something to say?"

"*Astaghfirullah,*" Amani said reluctantly, for she was not that sorry for what she had said. "But I still think he is."

"Thinking is different than saying," Grandma smiled. "Anyway, you might want to consider that there are many reasons why Mr. Carr may have been short with you both yesterday. Maybe he was tired from the move or missing his family. We just don't know."

"But we tried to be so nice to him. Hude cleaned up the cicadas. You and I baked him cookies. Mr. Carr doesn't even know what we did for him."

"But Allah knows what your intentions were and that's what counts," Grandma Hana said. "We always have a choice to do what is right in any given circumstance. With respect to Mr. Carr, we have a duty to treat him well because he is our neighbor, even if he is not particularly nice to us. Do you remember the story about the neighbor who used to try to annoy the Prophet, peace be upon him, by throwing garbage in his path? One day he walked out of his home but did not see anything. The Prophet wondered what had happened to the neighbor. He found out that she was sick and visited her. That's a great example of what it means to be a good neighbor and a good Muslim."

"It's hard to be nice to someone who isn't nice to you," Amani said.

"It is," Grandma Hana agreed. "It takes a lot of work to be a good person, and it's often hard to know what is right to do. That is why Allah tells us to follow the example of the Prophet, who is the best of creation, peace be upon him. If you think about it, a good person is like this peach tree. Why do you think the peach tree never fell down in any storm all of these years?"

"Because it has strong roots," Hude said.

"Exactly." Grandma Hana smiled. "Can you see the roots?"

"No," answered Hude.

"Even though we can't see them, we know they are there because the tree hasn't blown over. Strong roots keep the tree stable during storms. In the same way, our faith keeps us strong during difficult times.

"Who remembers the *Hadith* of Gabriel and the six principles of *iman*?"

"I do," Amani said. "We believe in Allah, His

angels, His books, His prophets, the Day of Judgment, and divine destiny."

"Can you see all of these things, Amani?"

"No, Grandma."

"Just like the roots of a tree, our beliefs keep us strong. There is more to our peach tree than just roots, isn't there?" Grandma Hana said.

"It also has a trunk, branches, leaves...," Hude said.

"And the peaches, of course!" Amani said.

"And we can see all of those," Grandma continued. "The trunk, branches, and leaves are our actions. All of the parts of the tree, both the visible and hidden, work together to produce the fruit, just as our actions and faith work together to produce good character."

"I don't understand, Grandma," Amani said.

"Here, think about it this way," Grandma Hana began to explain. "The trunk of the tree represents the *shahadah*. It is what someone says to become Muslim. 'I testify there is no God but God, and Muhammad is the Messenger of Allah.' But that is only the first action we take. It takes a lot more to be a good Muslim. What else are we required to do?"

"Praying five times a day, paying *zakah*, fasting during Ramadan, and performing the hajj, if we can," Hude said.

"Those four things that we do are the branches of the tree. What connects the roots and branches?"

"The trunk," Amani said.

"Exactly," Grandma Hana said. "And taking the *shahadah* connects our faith with our actions. We need both working together to make the tree healthy."

"What about the leaves, Grandma?" Amani asked.

"The leaves on a tree are the *Sunnah* of the Prophet, peace be upon him, how he taught us to act in all kinds of situations. The leaves are the things by which we recognize someone as Muslim. In the same way, we recognize a peach tree by its long slender leaves. When we say '*as-salamu 'alaykum*' and 'alhamdulillah', people know that we are Muslim."

"Don't forget the peaches!" Amani exclaimed.

"Not a chance," Grandma Hana said. "What is the main purpose of a peach tree?"

"To make a peach?" Hude said, not quiet sure of his answer.

"You're right. The roots, trunk, branches and leaves all work together to produce the fruit. In the same way, our faith and everything we do as a Muslim work together to help us to be a good person, the type of person that Allah created us to be. The fruits of Islam are such things as patience, honesty, kindness and generosity. Part of that is being nice to our neighbors, even if they are not nice to us."

"I think I get it now, Grandma," Amani said.

"And as you know, it's not always easy to do what is right, just as it is not easy to produce good fruit. Growing a fruit tree requires constant care."

"Like pruning," Hude said.

"That's right," Grandma Hana agreed. "A tree needs to be pruned. Developing good character needs constant attention as well. Pruning is like cutting out bad habits or anything *haram*.

"There is one more part of the tree that we haven't discussed. It's hidden, and we can plant it."

"The pit!" Amani blurted out.

"Right, and the pit is important because it has a seed inside it. And what protects the seed?" Grandma asked her grandson.

"The fruit," Hude answered.

"Just as a fruit protects the seed, good character protects our hearts. What does a seed grow into, Amani?"

"A new tree."

"In the same way, just like a seed grows into a tree, a sound heart gives new life to a person in *jannah*. Everything we do is to protect our hearts so we can be with Allah in *jannah*. But remember it is only with Allah's mercy that anyone gets to *jannah*. The Prophet Muhammad, peace be upon him, told his Companions that no one's good deeds would get them to *jannah* without Allah's mercy, even his own. He then said: '*Therefore, do good deeds properly, sincerely and moderately, and worship Allah in the forenoon and in the afternoon and during a part of the night, and always adopt a middle, moderate, regular course whereby you will reach your target.*'

"Hude, what is 'target' referring to here?" Grandma Hana asked.

"Target means paradise. It means that doing good deeds and worshipping Allah will help us to reach paradise."

"There's a lot we can learn from a tree, Grandma," Amani said.

"There certainly is, Amani. So, tell me. What do you both have planned for the rest of the day?"

"I'm hoping to practice with some new adjustments I made to my bow," Hude said. "The County Fair is just over a week away."

"Good character takes practice too," Grandma said. "And what about you, Amani?"

"I haven't written in my journal for days. And I want to get back to my book. Tad Walker is just about to save a totem pole from destruction."

"The famous Tad Walker is now saving dead trees?" Hude said.

"Not just any dead tree," Amani said. "It's a two thousand-year-old, sacred totem pole with a secret message on it. I think it leads to a treasure, but I'm not sure."

"Well, that's just silly," Hude commented.

"I don't think so. If you can learn so much from a live tree, why can't you learn something from a dead tree? Isn't that right, Grandma?"

Grandma smiled. "There is much to be learned from all of Allah's creation. In fact, everything in creation is sending us a message. Allah said: 'We will show them Our Signs in the universe, and in their own selves, until it becomes manifest to them that this is the truth.'"

"Everything, Grandma?"

"Yes, Amani. The wind, the moon, the stars, the seasons, shadows, everything," Grandma Hana said. "We just have to listen."

Preparations

HUDE looked out of the kitchen window. Pal was in Grandma Hana's backyard. He had something in his mouth and was swinging it around.

"Grandma, I'm going to get Pal. He wiggled out of his collar again."

"Thank you, honey," Grandma Hana stopped humming briefly to answer him.

She was at the sink, cleaning jars for canning peaches. She enjoyed preparing for the harvest almost as much as the harvest itself. Very soon they were going to be eating peaches several times a day—peach chutney, chilled peach soup, spicy baked peaches, peach ice cream, peach cobbler and, of course, peach pie.

"Pal, how did you get that this time? Amani will freak if she sees you with it. Don't tell her I told you, but she doesn't like you very much."

Hude walked over to the dog and petted him. He carefully removed Amani's backpack from his mouth and put it over his shoulder. For some reason, Pal loved that backpack.

A few days had gone by since Mr. Carr had moved in. They hadn't seen much of Mr. Carr, but they had seen plenty of Pal. Mr. Carr bought a long chain to keep Pal on his property. The problem was that Pal liked Grandma Hana's yard much better. Every chance he got, Pal wiggled out of his collar and took off. And he usually got into trouble. If he wasn't running through the flowerbeds chasing bees, he had something in his mouth that he should not have. Pal was a lot of work and he wasn't even their dog. But Hude didn't mind, except when he was trying to practice for the target archery competition.

In target archery, competitors shoot on a flat surface from a line that runs parallel to the target faces. The targets have multicolored circles that have a common center. There are a total of ten circles of increasing size. In the center of the target are two smaller gold circles, surrounded by two larger red circles, surrounded by two larger blue circles, surrounded by two larger black circles, and finally two larger white circles. Each circle has a point value. A shot in the smallest gold circle in the center, or bullseye, is worth 10 points. A shot in the outermost white circle scores 1 point. As the circles increase in size, the points assigned to them decrease. In indoor target tournaments, archers shoot from a distance of 25 meters or 18 meters. In the outdoor competitions the distances are greater: 30, 50, 70, and 90 meters.

The Fairfax County Fair was basically holding an indoor competition outdoors. Archers would be shooting from a distance of 18 meters in an outside range. The fairgrounds didn't have an indoor facility or enough space outside for the longer distances. But although the distance to the target was shorter like an indoor competition, there was still the wind factor of an outdoor competition.

Grandma Hana's yard made a perfect target practicing range for this competition. It was mostly flat, except for a slight rise near the end of the backyard leading to the peach tree. But that was almost 40 meters from the house, leaving more than enough room to shoot at a target 18 meters across a flat surface. Since it was outside, Hude also had the advantage of practicing with wind conditions.

All archers were required to use a barebow recurve. Barebow archery is about as simple as it gets. The bow cannot have sights, stabilizers, or a draw check indicator to let the archer know when the arrow has been drawn back far enough. Kisser buttons, a plastic button mounted on the bowstring that touches the upper lip when the bow is drawn, were not allowed. The only extras that could be added to the bow were an arrow rest and one nocking point, a place on the bowstring where the back end of the arrow is fastened before release. Archers were allowed a finger protector for the draw fingers, as well as an arm guard to protect the skin from the bowstring and a chest guard to provide a flat, smooth surface for the string to slide over.

With a recurve bow the tips of the bow curve away from the archer when the bow is held in a shooting position. The shape allows the bow to store more energy. Because the bowstring is under a much higher tension, the arrow goes farther when shot. Hude liked using a recurve bow. It was the type of bow used by Muslims since the beginning of Islam.

There were no restrictions on the type of arrows that could be used. That was left to the judgment of the individual archers.

Hude's bow was a fifty inch recurve from limb to limb, with a draw weight of twenty pounds. The bow had Curly Black Walnut limbs and a Curly Black Walnut and Maple riser. It was a beautiful bow, both in performance and appearance. His grandfather had made it for him before he died. Hude used 9.33 millimeter aluminum arrows with natural feather fletching. He used a leather finger tab, and wore an arm guard and a chest guard.

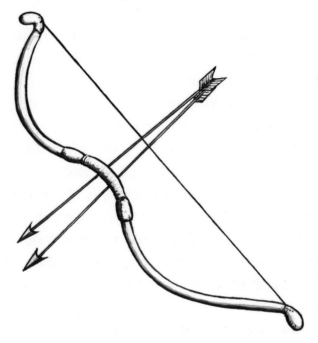

As Hude prepared for the archery competition, Amani and Grandma Hana prepared to make pie. This was Amani's first pie contest, and the first time Grandma Hana had a partner. Grandma Hana told Amani that now that she was an official baker, she would have to make some of the important cooking decisions herself. This was a huge responsibility. What if they lost? It would be all her fault. Grandma Hana told her not to worry. The peach tree had already done the hard work. Her secret to winning was to do as little as possible to the peaches. The decisions would have to be made in the crust.

"Grandma, do you have anything special planned tomorrow?" Hude said when he came inside late that morning.

Grandma Hana and Amani were sitting in the same two spots as when he left.

"We were hoping to go to the lake and see if our tree swing is still there," he said.

"Sounds like a perfect way to spend a summer day. You might meet some other kids at the lake. Mr. Fenby told me that they built some new homes where the field used to be."

"I hope they're nicer than those boys who were on the train," Amani said.

She had told her Grandma Hana all about Bobby and his friends the night they arrived.

Bobby!

Amani suddenly remembered the name of the boy who threw the cicada at her.

Could it be? Could he be the same Bobby McPherson who Mr. Fenby was talking about a few days ago?

Sabotage

Tad Walker ran as fast as he could through the thick jungle. Poison arrows flew all around him. He had two choices. Neither of them was good. He could either jump in the canoe and head down the rapids, risking falling into the river with its giant man-eating fish. Or, he could climb up the two thousand foot vertical cliff face without any ropes to stop him from falling. As always, he chose to...

"Amani, let's go! You can bring the book with you."

It was the third time Hude had called for her. After about an hour of practicing in the scorching heat, he was more than ready for a swim.

Good idea, Amani thought to herself.

She quickly shoved the book into her backpack. Already packed inside were Mr.

Panda, Band-Aids, a pen, a water bottle, and Crickety Crunch, a snack that could only be bought at the Reading Terminal Market in Philadelphia. As she was leaving her room, she noticed her grandmother's peach pie recipe on top of her dresser. The paper had turned a yellowish-brown from age and the handwriting was so faint, it was barely legible. Amani carefully folded the recipe and placed it in an inside pocket of her backpack. She wanted to study it at the lake. Her journal lay on her bed, forgotten.

"I'm coming. I'm coming," she called.

Amani hurried down the stairs. Hude was waiting for her at the front door.

"About time," he muttered. "Here, can I put these in your backpack?"

Hude handed her their grandfather's archery notebook and his handheld video game. Amani looked at him with another look he knew well.

"What?" Hude said defensively. "Mama and Baba said I couldn't play any video games at Grandma's house. They didn't say anything about the lake."

"But you know that's what they meant," Amani pointed out.

"But that's not what they said."

Hude took the backpack from Amani and packed his things inside it.

"Let's go. It's late already," Hude said.

"I remember that hill being a lot bigger," Amani commented as they walked along the path that led to the lake.

"That's because we were a lot smaller," Hude said. "Remember how scared we used to be near this part. We thought there were trolls living over there."

"That's right! I forgot completely about the trolls," Amani laughed. "Stop, for a second." Amani grabbed Hude's hand. "Did you hear that?"

"Hear what? Trolls?" he laughed.

"No, I'm serious. I thought I heard voices."

Hude listened for a few seconds.

"I don't hear anything. If it's anyone, it's probably just kids from the new development. No big deal."

A few minutes later they were at the lake.

"It's still here!" Hude said happily.

Their Baba had chosen the perfect tree to set up the rope swing. The tree sat on a small hill near the edge of the lake. They would run down the hill, fly into the air and land in the water.

"But that's new," Amani said.

In another tree not too far away, someone had built a tree fort.

"Wow, that's high. Isn't it?" Hude commented.

"Too high for me. That's for sure," Amani said.

Amani didn't like heights, along with not liking bugs. Reading about Tad Walker's insect and climbing adventures was enough for her.

"Anyway, it's not ours," Hude said. "I call the swing first."

Hude grabbed the end of the thick rope. It had a large knot on it. The other end was tied to one of the higher branches in the tree. He walked up the hill, holding on to the rope. He ran down as fast as he could, and swung high into the air. When he was over the water, he let go. He landed in the lake with a big splash.

"This feels great," he said when his head popped out of the water.

"My turn!" Amani said.

She put her backpack down and ran up the hill. She also landed with a big splash.

"I'm starting from farther up this time," Hude announced.

He flew even higher in the air and landed with an even bigger splash, but something felt wrong.

"That was weird," he said when he surfaced.

"What was weird?" Amani asked. "It looked

pretty good to me."

"Just before I let go, I dropped a couple of inches. That's never happened before."

"The rope was probably tangled and straightened itself out," Amani said. "Anyway, it's my turn."

Amani grabbed the rope and climbed up the hill, almost as far as Hude. She ran down as fast as she could, passing Hude on his way up.

Snap!

Hude heard a loud sound and heavy splash in the water. The thick rope had crashed down on top of Amani. She was tangled up in it and her head was underwater.

Hude started running down the hill to help her but he tripped. He tumbled head-over-heels until he hit the water. Amani still had not surfaced.

"Amani, Amani!" he yelled, thrashing his way towards her. He grabbed whatever he could find and pulled it to the surface. Amani tried to catch her breath, as he dragged her to the shore. The rope was still wrapped around her.

"Are you okay?" he asked.

"I'm fine. I'm fine," she said, trying to catch her breath. "I couldn't figure out which way was up. The rope kept pulling me under. That was terrifying."

"You're telling me!" Hude said.

Hude plopped himself on the ground. His heart thumped loudly in his chest. Amani walked over to get the fallen rope.

"Look at this," she called back to Hude from the water. "Someone did this on purpose."

Amani walked back and handed Hude the end of the rope that had snapped. It had been cut with a knife part of the way through.

"Did you hear that, Bobby?" a boy laughed from the tree fort. "Someone did this on purpose," he said, mocking Amani.

Hude and Amani looked up. Three boys were standing outside the tree fort on a platform. It was the boy named Bobby and his two friends from the train. Bobby was holding a bow.

"That wasn't funny. Someone could get hurt," Amani yelled to them.

"By someone, do you mean you?" the boy said.

"See, it's funny. We're laughing," another boy said.

Hude was really angry, but he remembered what the Prophet said about who is truly strong. The strong person is not the one who uses his strength to overcome someone else, but the one who controls himself when angry. His Baba also told him that sometimes it is better to walk away. And this was one of those times. No good could come from fighting with these boys in the woods.

"Just ignore them, Amani," Hude told her. "It's not worth it. We'll come back later and fix the tree swing. Mr. Fenby will help us."

"Why should we leave?" Amani said. "We have just as much right to be here as they do. I want to swim."

"Swim if you like," Hude said. "But I think it's a bad idea."

Amani jumped in the water.

"This feels great, Hude. You should join me."

"Hey, you," one of the boys yelled from the tree fort. "Tell your sister she can't swim here. This is our swimming hole."

Amani was about to respond but Hude stopped her.

"I'm telling you to ignore them. They are just trying to pick a fight."

"Did you hear him?" the other boy shouted. "We are telling you to leave!"

The boy had a stone in his hand and was tossing it up in the air and catching it.

"I heard you. But I'm not leaving!" Amani yelled back from the water.

"Really?" the boy with the stone said.

Without warning, he threw the stone at Amani. It didn't hit her but it was close enough.

"Hey," Hude said in angry tone. "Don't do that again."

"Or what? Are you going to stop me?"

The three boys laughed. Hude saw a large stone on the ground near him. He thought about picking it up but decided against it.

"Let's go, Amani."

This time she agreed. She started towards her backpack. The same boy took another stone from a pile on the platform and threw it at her.

It didn't hit her either, but the point had been made. They wanted a fight.

"Let's just go, Hude," she said when her brother's face turned red. "We can be halfway home by the time they get down from the tree fort."

"I remember you from the train," Bobby said. "I saw you carrying a bow case."

"Instead of playing with pebbles, why don't we settle this Saturday at the Fair," Hude said calmly, although he was very angry.

"You know I'm a pretty good aim. Watch this."

Bobby placed an arrow in the bow he was holding, pulled back and aimed at a makeshift target that had been hung on a tree on the other side of the lake. The arrow flew through the air and landed a little off from the center.

"That's okay, but I've seen better," Hude said.

"Oh, you think you can beat me?" Bobby asked.

"I think I can," Hude said confidently.

"Okay. The Fair it is. We'll see who's the better shot."

"Yes, we will." Hude turned to Amani and whispered, "Let's go now."

Hude grabbed Amani's hand and they started to walk away.

"That's it, Bobby? The Fair?" the boy who had been throwing the stones said. "That might be good enough for you, but I don't want to wait. I'm settling this now."

He took a rope that was tied to the tree and flung it over the platform.

"Are you guys, coming?" he said to Bobby and the other boy.

Hude looked back. One boy was half way down the rope, and Bobby and the third boy were waiting on the platform to follow.

"Amani, as soon as we get on the path, run as fast as you can."

Amani didn't have to be told twice. Once she started running she didn't stop until they reached their grandmother's property. "Hude, please give me some water out of the backpack. I'm so thirsty," Amani said. She was bent over, resting her hands on her knees and breathing heavily.

"I don't have the backpack. I thought you had it," Hude said.

"But I thought you had it. My book is in there. And my panda! And Grandma's recipe! I didn't even ask her if I could take it with me!"

"Grandpop's notebook is in there too and … I can't believe it, my video game! Why did I ever take it with me? That was so dumb."

"We have to go back. Right now!" Amani pleaded.

"We can't go back now. Those boys are probably still there."

"But we have to try," Amani said.

"We'll go back tomorrow. We'll look for it then."

"This day couldn't get any worse," Amani said as they walked toward the house.

But she was wrong.

Good fences
don't always make
good neighbors

GRANDMA Hana was in the backyard near the peach tree talking to Mr. Fenby. Both of them were acting strangely. Mr. Fenby was fidgeting with his hat in his hand. His head was bent down and he was staring at the ground. Grandma Hana's arms were folded in front of her and she had a serious look on her face.

"What's going on Grandma?" Hude said as they approached.

Amani didn't say anything, but she knew something was wrong.

Grandma Hana hesitated for a moment.

"It seems that our peach tree is definitely on Mr. Carr's property. Mr. Fenby double-checked with the county. It also seems that Mr. Carr still wants to put a fence around his property."

"So, that's okay. Isn't it Grandma? Mr. Carr could put the fence a few feet back." Amani asked.

Hude said nothing. He knew what was coming.

"Unfortunately, Amani...," Grandma Hana paused. "Unfortunately, Mr. Carr does not want to do that."

"What does that mean, Grandma? What does that mean?" Amani said.

"I'm afraid it means that he wants to cut down the peach tree," Grandma Hana said.

"He wants to cut down the tree?" Amani shouted. "That's not fair! Mr. Carr is so mean. Well, he's not going to do it. I won't let him!"

"Sweetheart," Grandma said lovingly, "everything will be okay, alhamdulillah. We will get through this."

"I won't let him do it, Grandma. I won't let him!" Amani said through a waterfall of tears. "Mr. Fenby, you have to stop him. Please, stop him!"

"I tried, Amani. I tried. He just wouldn't listen to reason. I even asked him if he would sell that part of his property. He won't budge."

"Can't you move the tree then?" Amani asked.

"It's too old and too big. It would die if we tried to move it," Mr. Fenby said.

"Amani, Mr. Fenby has done all that he can," Grandma Hana started to explain. "Mr. Carr wanted the peach tree cut down today. Mr. Fenby convinced him to wait until Sunday, after the pie contest."

"I also told him that he could hire someone else to put up his fence," Mr. Fenby added. "I can't bear to do it. I tried, Hana. I really tried to save the peach tree."

"I know you did. We all know you did," Grandma Hana told him. "Amani, we will save a pit from this year's harvest and plant a new peach tree in the middle of the yard."

"It's not the same. It's not the same," Amani cried.

Grandma Hana pulled Amani close and held her tight. Amani buried her face in her grandmother's arms and sobbed.

The plan

AFTER crying herself to sleep the night before, Amani woke up more determined than she had ever been. If Tad Walker could save a dead tree, she certainly could save one that was still alive.

"Hude, I have a plan to save the peach tree!" Amani jumped on his bed.

"I'm sleeping. Tell me later."

"No you're not. Now get up. We're going on a bike ride."

Amani pulled the pillow from under Hude's head. His head flopped back down on the bed. Hude turned around and sat up.

"I thought you wanted to look for your backpack today?"

"Today we are going to save the tree. Tomorrow Mr. Panda. Let's go. We don't have any time to waste."

Amani threw his pillow back at him and went downstairs.

"Grandma, may Hude and I bike to town? There is something I want to do there."

Grandma Hana looked at Amani curiously.

"Of course. You might have to fill the tires, but otherwise I think the bikes are okay. What put you in such a good mood this morning?"

"I decided that I can either sit around and cry about the peach tree, or try to do something to save it."

Grandma Hana smiled at Amani. She loved her spunk, but was worried that her granddaughter would get hurt. Saving the peach tree wasn't going to be easy. Grandma Hana had been up most of the night thinking about it. She hadn't come up with any good ideas.

"Remember, Amani: no matter what happens, we can plant another peach tree. We'll save the pit from the first peach picked this year and we'll plant it. In a few years, we'll have peaches again, inshallah."

"There will never be a peach tree like that one, Grandma."

Amani pointed out of the kitchen window to the majestic tree in the backyard.

"She never looks more beautiful than at harvest time," Amani said.

Grandma Hana agreed. The tree was in all her glory.

"Well, let's go!" Hude said, grabbing an apple from the fruit bowl on the counter. "I have to put in two practices today."

Amani couldn't wait to ride her mother's childhood bike. It was an old, pink Stingray with a long banana seat and a big, white plastic basket with purple plastic flowers. It was heavy and had only one gear. Amani felt like a real country girl riding it. Grandpop's bike was ancient as well. Hude, on the other hand, would have preferred to be riding his friend's new 21-speed, lightweight mountain bike with shock absorbers.

"Where are we going and what are we doing?" Hude called to Amani as they turned off Sycamore Street.

"We are going to the mayor's office and we are going to ask him to save our tree," she said with confidence.

It took twenty minutes to ride to downtown Cherry Hill, if you could call it that. There wasn't much there. Almost everything—the post office, the corner store, the hardware store, the diner, the town dentist, the school, the fire station, and the mayor's office—was located on Main Street. Main Street turned into Route 45 as soon as the town limits were passed. On the way, they passed the county fairgrounds.

"There it is," said Amani. "I remember it from one of Grandma's photos."

Amani pointed to a small but noble building. It was made of solid brick and rested on the top of twenty white marble steps. They dropped their bikes on the sidewalk, not worrying about if they would be stolen. Amani ran up the steps first. Hude followed walking. Amani tried to open the large, wooden double doors but they were too heavy. Hude had to help her. Inside was absolutely quiet. There was no one around, not even a police officer. A sign stated that the mayor's office was located on the second floor.

There was a door at the top of the stairs with the name 'Mayor Spencer Mathews' on it. They knocked and a voice told them to come in.

"Well, hello. How can I help you?" A woman about their Grandma's age greeted them.

"We have come to see Mayor Mathews," Amani said calmly.

The woman smiled at Amani. "Well, let me check if the mayor is able to see you now. I know he's about to leave in a few minutes. What are your names?"

"Amani."

"Hude."

About thirty seconds later, she returned with the mayor. He was a heavyset man, and his large belly hung comfortably over his belt. He held a jacket in his left hand and extended his right.

"Nice to meet you, Hude and Amani," he said, shaking their hands. "Dixie tells me you want to see me. How can I help?"

"My Grandma has a very special tree that we just found out is on the neighbor's property," Amani began to explain. "The neighbor wants to cut it down right after the County Fair, so he can put up a fence. We want to know how we can stop him."

"Hmm, you do have a problem. Are you sure that the tree is on his property?" the mayor asked.

"Very sure," Amani said.

"Has your grandmother asked him to sell that part of his property to her?"

"He won't sell it," Hude said. "And he won't even move the fence a few feet back."

"I'm very sorry kids, but I don't think there is anything I can do. It's his property. He can do what he wants with it. I wish I had something better to tell you," the mayor said as put his jacket on. "Dixie, I'm going to meet the fire chief at the fairgrounds. I should be back before lunch. Bye kids."

"What are we going to do now?" Amani asked Hude.

"I don't know. We'll think of something. There is prize money for winning the archery competition. Perhaps Mr. Carr will change his mind and sell the property."

Dixie could see the disappointment on the kids' faces as they tried to figure out what to do. She had grandchildren about the same age.

"Didn't you say that the tree was special?" Dixie asked.

"Very special," said Amani.

"In what way is it special?" she asked.

Amani thought a moment.

"In so many ways. It is the oldest peach tree that I know that still produces fruit. It was supposed to be a nectarine tree. It makes the best peach pies. My Grandma always wins first prize at the County Fair. And it's a great teacher. It is...."

"Did you say first prize at the County Fair?" Dixie said. "You wouldn't happen to be Hana Brenner's grandkids?"

"We are," Amani said.

"I went to school with your grandfather. He was a good man. I remember when he brought Hana home from Turkey as his wife. This small town had never seen anything quite like her. We all fell in love with her in no time. I've been looking forward to a piece of her pie for months now. Now, who on earth would want to cut down that tree? There must be something wrong with him. Or, maybe he just hasn't tried Hana's pie."

"Or maybe he's just plain old mean," Amani said.

"Amani, that's backbiting. You shouldn't say that," Hude whispered to her.

Amani knew Hude was right but she didn't feel like saying what she knew she should.

"I'll tell you what kids," Dixie said. "Let me make a few calls. Come back in about an hour. You should go down to the fairgrounds. They're setting up for Saturday and sometimes they'll even let you try some of the rides."

"I'll race you there," Hude said as soon as they got on the bikes.

"That's not fair," Amani said when she arrived at the fairgrounds after him. "Your bike has three gears."

"Haven't you figured out by now that life isn't always fair?" Hude said.

Amani thought about what Hude had said. She thought about Bobby McPherson and the tree swing. She thought about Grandma Hana and Mr. Carr. She thought about Mr. Panda, all alone in her backpack. Hude was right. Life isn't always fair.

"Hey, that looks like fun," Hude said, pointing to a bunch of old-fashioned looking bikes. The sign for the ride said 'Hi-Wheels Derby'. The hi-wheel bikes had a big wheel in the front and a tiny wheel in the back like a penny-farthing, but were kid-sized. A few kids were trying to ride them. They kept losing their balance and laughing.

Hude tried it first. It didn't ride like a regular bike. It was much harder to stay up, but it was fun. After falling off a few times he seemed to get the hang of it. He was soon riding faster than any kid there. Amani tried next. She only fell off once because Hude had taught her how to ride.

"What do you think is behind that fence?" Amani asked when they were finished with the hi-wheels.

"I don't know but I'll find out."

Hude jumped up and pulled himself over the fence to see. He quickly dropped down.

"They're having target practice down there. And I think I see Bobby McPherson and his brother! Let's go around the other side. I saw a place we can watch without being seen."

Hude and Amani crouched behind some bushes on a hill above the shooting range. It was definitely Bobby McPherson. The older boy looked like it could be his brother.

"What do you think? Can you beat them?" Amani said after a few minutes of watching.

"I don't know. They're both really good. The older boy seems to have more confidence and strength, but Bobby has better form. See the position of the older brother's feet. It's called an open stance. His foot closest to the target is father away from the target line than his other foot. Usually only experienced archers try that. It's easy to turn your chest toward the target and mess up your whole shot."

"Hey, you two," a young man who looked in his late teens called from the bottom of the hill. "You're not supposed to be up there."

The man was sitting in a golf cart at the top of a paved path that disappeared into a field. Next to the path was a sign. It read 'Cycling Track'.

"Sorry, we didn't know," Amani said.

"We should leave anyway," Hude said. "Maybe Miss Dixie has figured something out."

"I hope so," Amani said.

Hude and Amani crouched down as they walked down the hill to get their bikes.

"Before we leave, I want to check out the cycling track over there," Hude said. "I've seen track cycling on ESPN. The track has banks. Some of the banks are really high. It's crazy."

"That sounds like fun," Amani said. "Maybe there will be races to watch at the Fair."

"I don't want to watch. I want to race myself," Hude said.

Hude and Amani rode their bikes to the entrance of the track. The man on the golf cart was gone. A little bit ahead on the path was a strip of yellow plastic with the word 'Caution' written on it, so they couldn't go any farther. Fifteen minutes later they were knocking on the door to the mayor's office.

"Come in," Dixie said.

Amani and Hude open the door and walked inside the room. Dixie was sitting at her desk.

They couldn't tell by her expression whether the news was good or bad.

"To be honest, at first I didn't find much. I made a lot of calls, but no one could think of anything. I was staring at the wall, deciding what to do next, when I saw that photo of the mayor standing in front of the Wye Oak tree. Do you know what that was?"

Hude and Amani both answered no.

"It was a gigantic white oak tree in Talbot County, the largest of its kind in the nation. It was believed to have been around since the 1500s, long before this country was an English colony. In 2002, it fell down in a severe thunderstorm. That photo on the wall is the mayor in front of the tree a few years before it toppled over."

Hude and Amani looked at the photograph more closely. The tree was enormous. Mayor Mathews stood proudly, like the tree itself.

"It was part of the Maryland Big Tree Program and a national champion for over forty years," Dixie said. "The State of Maryland purchased the tree from its owner because of its historical and outstanding interest. It was declared Maryland's State Tree. The Wye Oak State Park was established to protect the tree. Marylanders love their trees."

"But Grandma's peach tree isn't nearly that big," Hude said.

"No, it isn't," Dixie said. "It may not be a national champion, but your Grandmom's peach tree has an historical and outstanding interest to Fairfax County. The Wye Oak tree gave me an idea. I called the mayor and he immediately called the County Commissioner. We want to declare your grandmother's peach tree a symbol of Fairfax County. The County will buy the tree and the thin strip of property underneath it—with donations of course. Your neighbor may not want to sell it now, but it will be difficult for him not to sell when he sees the proclamation declaring the peach tree a county treasure."

"It's perfect!" Amani said excitedly.

"It is," Hude agreed.

"There's just one problem," Dixie said in a serious tone. "This cannot be accomplished by Sunday. The County Commissioner thinks he can get it through next week. Until that time you are going to have to make sure that your neighbor doesn't cut down that tree. And you can't mention the plan to anyone, except your grandmother, of course. It will be easier to get it through if not a lot of people are involved."

Hude and Amani looked at each other to see if the other one had any ideas. Neither said anything. "Don't worry, Miss Dixie," Amani finally said. "We'll figure something out. We won't let Mr. Carr cut down that tree, even if we have to live in it for a week!"

Hude and Amani ran down both sets of stairs. They picked up their bikes and straddled them and stood there talking.

"Hude, how are we going to stop Mr. Carr from cutting down the tree?"

"You already figured it out," Hude said. "We are going to live in it!"

"We can't live in it for a week," Amani said.

"We don't have to," Hude said. "Mr. Carr isn't planning to cut the tree down until Sunday, after the County Fair. We'll take turns sitting in the tree, 24/7, until that proclamation comes. He can't cut down a tree with a kid in it. I think it can work."

"It has to. It just has to," Amani said.

"Wow!" said Hude. "Turn around and check that out."

Pink petals swirled upwards in the air and across a thin strip of grass between the sidewalk and the street. It looked like a two foot toy tornado. A gust of wind then nearly knocked them off their bikes. Amani looked around. The light green underside of the leaves could be seen. She noticed the sky. It was black to the west.

"We better get home quickly," she said. "The wind's telling us that it's going to storm."

The storm

"OH, NO!" Amani called out. "Hude, wait up. I think my tire is flat. We'll never make it home before the storm now."

They stopped riding and Hude looked at the tire.

"It's not flat, but it is low. There's the corner store. Maybe we can put more air in it there."

A few minutes later Hude was walking out of the store with a bicycle pump in his hand.

"Luckily for us, Wylie, some kid behind the counter, bikes as well. He let me borrow this."

Hude pumped air in the tire and checked for leaks.

"This should get you home," Hude said.

Clunk!

"What's that noise?" Hude asked. *Clunk ... clunk ... clunk. Clunk ... clunk.*

"It's hail!" Amani screamed.

Hude and Amani grabbed their bikes and ran under a metal awning. Hail, the size of large marbles, struck from the sky. The constant pounding sounded as if they were inside a large drum.

"I don't believe it," Amani said. "The hail is denting the roof."

"It's a good thing your tire needed air. We could have been riding our bikes in this. If one of these landed on your head, it might kill you. Look at the corn over there. It's completely pummeled."

"The peach tree!" Amani shouted.

Less than a minute later, it was oddly silent. The hailstorm stopped as abruptly as it had started. The sun came out and started melting the hailstones.

They returned the pump to Wylie at the corner store and started home. They wanted to get home quickly to see if the peach tree was okay. People everywhere were inspecting the damage from the storm. A car had been abandoned on the side of the road. Cracks in the windshield formed the shape of a large spiderweb. A plastic awning over a porch was shredded to pieces. Chairs and tables were overturned, flowerbeds leveled.

"Oh, no! The road's closed," Amani said. "What now?"

"Let's go back and ask that kid at the store

if there's another way home. He was helpful before."

Wylie was cleaning up from the storm when they arrived.

"Excuse me," Hude said. "The main road is closed. We need to get to 494 Sycamore. Do you know a back way?"

"You were just at the fairgrounds, weren't you?" Wiley said, remembering the conversation he had had with Hude.

"Yes," said Hude.

"I know only one other way to get to Sycamore Street from here. You will have to go back to the fairgrounds. Near the archery range is a new cycle track.

"We saw it," Amani said. "Isn't it closed?"

"Don't worry about it," Wiley told them. "The tape's there to keep younger kids away. My friends and I use it all the time. Just don't be too obvious or someone will stop you. The track has two routes. A circular track and another track that winds down a big hill. Take the windy one down. Don't go too fast. It's quite a ride and that track isn't finished yet. The track will dump you onto an unpaved path that is behind some houses being built. That path leads to a bridge over a stream. Not far after the bridge the path will put you at the very end of Sycamore Street. Make a left and you're there. It's actually faster than using the main road. I use it a lot. It's awesome going down, not so much fun pedaling up."

Hude and Amani rode as fast as they could to the fairgrounds. Strangely, there was no sign of a storm there. They slipped under the caution tape and headed down the track.

"This is uber fun!" Hude screamed.

He was high on the bank of the track, winding down the hill at a fast speed. Amani mostly stayed on the flat part of the track until near the end. The track abruptly ended. They both almost lost their balance when they hit the unpaved dirt.

"What's that up ahead," Amani said after they had been riding a few minutes.

"I think it's a little dog," Hude said.

A whitish shih-tzu mix, not more than seven pounds, was blocking the path in front of them. She started yapping frantically as they approached, but she did not move.

"She's so cute. Not like that drooling machine that lives behind us," Amani said. "What would she be doing out here all by herself? She must be lost."

"Check to see if she has a collar," Hude said.

Amani got off her bike and walked closer to the little dog.

"I don't see a collar. Maybe we should take her home and put some signs up that we found her. The dog will fit in my basket."

Amani bent down to pick up the dog but immediately jumped back.

"She tried to bite me!"

The dog was now off the path but still yapping.

"Look out!" Hude said.

All of sudden the little dog charged Amani. As she ran to her bike, the dog nipped at her feet. She jumped on her bike and rode away. The little dog chased her for a while. Hude didn't stop laughing until they arrived at the bridge.

"I think I'd rather swing across on that rope over there than ride on this," Hude said when he saw the bridge.

The bridge was falling apart. It was slanted to one side and several planks were missing.

"The rope swing doesn't look much better," Amani said, remembering her recent fiasco at the lake. "Look it's frayed at the top and could rip at any moment. Anyway, we have bikes. And who knows what's in that stream. You can't even see the bottom. I don't want to fall in it. Let's just walk our bikes across the bridge."

Hude agreed. About a minute or so later they were at the end of Sycamore Street. At first, there wasn't much storm damage. But the closer they got to their grandmother's house, the more damage they saw. At one point, they stopped to remove a thick branch from the road, reminding each other that it was a good deed. It didn't look good for the peaches.

They really started to worry when they were a few houses away. Mrs. Ryan's porch chair was in Grandma Hana's front lawn. A heavy branch had fallen on the roof and knocked off some shingles. Plant parts littered the property. They threw down their bikes and ran to the backyard. Grandma Hana had just walked onto the patio.

"How's the peach tree?" Amani asked between breaths. "We thought it would be destroyed. The hail was so big where we were."

"There was no hail here, alhamdulillah," Grandma Hana said. "That's a sturdy old peach tree. Strong roots. I didn't think she'd make it through the freeze of '99 or the brown rot of 2003. Looks like she's weathered this storm as well. Let's get closer and see if there's any damage."

Although a few of the smaller branches had broken off and peaches were lost, the tree was in good shape. The same could not be said about the yard. The patio furniture had been rearranged on the lawn. Leaves and branches were everywhere, including a large limb from a maple tree. And the roof looked even more damaged than in the front.

Grandma Hana and Amani started picking up the unripe peaches from the ground. Meanwhile, Hude started on the branches. He asked Grandma Hana and Amani to help him with the maple branch. But even the three of them working together could not move it. Mr. Carr was in his backyard. He saw them struggling with the branch, but he did not offer to help. Eventually, they gave up.

"Hude, would you please return this to Mr. Carr?"

Grandma Hana held Pal's favorite hard rubber red Kong toy in her hand.

"I think we should throw it away," Amani said. "That dog shouldn't be over here anyway. Why can't he keep *his* dog on *his* property? Anyone could see that the dog needs a smaller collar. Mr. Carr's just mean.

"*Astaghfirullah*," Amani added without being reminded.

"Amani, you don't have to like Mr. Carr, but you do have to be a good neighbor."

"I know, Grandma. I'm sorry. But I don't like that dog."

"You don't have to like the dog. But he is one of Allah's creations. Remember the man who gave a thirsty dog a drink and was promised paradise? Another man who did the same thing had his sins forgiven. Some of the Companions asked if there was a reward for serving animals. The Prophet, peace be upon him, told them, '*Yes, there is a reward for serving any living being*'. There are many examples of the Prophet, peace be upon him, teaching us to be kind to animals. We may not own a dog as a pet but our neighbor does. Why don't you go with Hude to return the toy? You'll be following a bad deed with a good."

Hude and Amani walked to Mr. Carr who was on his back deck, clearing some fallen branches.

"Mr. Carr, we don't want to bother you, but my Grandma asked us to return this to you. It's Pal's toy," Hude said.

"Just throw it over there, near the chain," said Mr. Carr.

Hude noticed an empty collar on the ground.

"You didn't happen to see Pal, did you?" Mr. Carr asked. "He took off in the storm. Last I saw him he was running into the woods."

"No. But if we do find him, we'll bring him back," Hude said.

"I'd appreciate it. My son loves that dog. He'll be upset if the dog's not here when he comes in a few days."

"Well, that wasn't too bad," Amani said as they walked back to Grandma Hana's house, stepping over the large maple branch on the way.

Saving Mr. Panda

AMANI woke up the next morning in an excellent mood. Mr. Fenby had stopped by yesterday after the storm. He and Hude removed the large maple branch from the backyard and they fixed the roof. Amani also told Grandma Hana that they had a plan to save the peach tree. But she didn't tell her any details. She wanted it to be a surprise. And today was the day they were going to save Mr. Panda. If Pal wasn't still missing, everything would be back to normal. Or at least, normal as they had come to know it.

"Good morning, Grandma. Lovely day, isn't it," Amani said when she entered the kitchen.

"Indeed it is."

"Are those sandwiches for us?" Amani asked.

"They are," Grandma said. "Hude asked me to make some. He said that the tree swing is broken and you want to fix it. I was going to put these in your backpack but I haven't seen it anywhere. Do you think Pal took it again?"

Hude and Amani had not yet told Grandma Hana about what happened at the lake. Hude said she had enough to worry about, what with the peach tree. In any event, it would all be settled one way or another at the archery competition in a few days.

"Pal didn't take it," Amani said truthfully. "Where's Hude? We have to leave for the lake."

"He's outside in the backyard. He's been working on something since *Fajr*. It must be important. He hasn't stopped, even for breakfast."

Amani walked out of the kitchen door to the back patio.

On the patio lay some sort of arrow contraption. The tip was a red toy suction cup, vaguely familiar. The shaft itself looked about the same as Hude's regular arrow to Amani, but connected to it was a partially unrolled piece of paper with the word 'test' written on it in Hude's sloppy handwriting.

Hude ran up to the patio and picked up the arrow.

"I just can't get it right. It's not going as far as I need it to go and it's not very accurate. Sorry that arrow nearly hit you. I didn't know you were coming outside."

"What are you trying to do, anyway?" Amani asked.

"I'm trying to shoot this arrow from the peach tree to the back of the house. It's about forty meters, I'm guessing. The shot isn't level because the peach tree is on that bump. It's more like field archery than target archery, and the suction cup is new so I'm having trouble aiming."

"I guess the question really is, *why* are you doing that?" Amani said.

"I was thinking about this all last night," Hude began. "If we are going to live in the peach tree, we need a way to communicate. What if I'm in the tree and I'm hungry or need to go the bathroom? We have to be able to get messages to each other without leaving the tree."

"Couldn't we just use Grandma's cell phone?"

"I thought about that, but what if the service is down?" Hude said.

"But how does this help me getting messages to you? Are you planning to teach me how to shoot arrows before Sunday?" Amani asked, still not quite sure about Hude's idea.

"Huh," Hude said, "I didn't think about that."

"We could also just yell for each other," Amani reminded him.

Hude looked annoyed.

"You do what you want to do. I'm going to use the bow," he said.

"Anyway," Amani said. "We don't have time for this now. Mr. Panda needs saving."

"What time is it?" Hude asked.

"It's almost nine o'clock."

"No wonder I'm starving," Hude said. "I'll work on this more when we get back."

Hude quickly collected his archery equipment. He put the arrow in his arrow case with the others. They ate home-made blueberry pancakes, made with Mrs. Ryan's blueberries, and then left for the lake.

"Do you hear anyone? I can't." Amani said, as they got closer to the lake.

"Not a thing, but we can't be too sure. We didn't know they were in the tree fort the last time."

Hude and Amani stopped near the end of the path to listen. After a few minutes of hearing only the sounds of the forest, they walked slowly to the tree that used to have the rope swing. The broken rope was still on the ground.

"I don't see my backpack anywhere," Amani said.

"Neither do I."

They searched all around the area but there was still no sign of the backpack. Hude looked over at the tree fort.

"I hate to say this, but I think we have to check the tree fort," Hude said.

"You mean *you* have to check the tree fort. I'm not climbing up that thing."

"Okay. *I* have to climb the tree fort. Do you think you could hold the rope steady while I climb it?"

"Yes," Amani said.

Hude climbed the rope up to the tree fort. It was even higher than it looked. All of a sudden, voices!

"Did you hear that, Amani?" Hude called down to her.

"What?" she listened for a few seconds. "They're coming! What are we going to do?"

"Go hide somewhere, and quick," Hude said.

Amani looked all around.

"There's no place good to hide. Come down and let's hide together. You don't want to be up there when they come, anyway."

"That's true," Hude said. "I hadn't thought of that. But let me check inside the fort for the backpack first."

Amani waited and waited for an eternity. At least it seemed that way to her. The voices were growing louder and she could now recognize one of them. Bobby McPherson. She had two choices. Neither of them was good. She could either stay on the ground and hide, and risk facing Bobby and his gang alone. Or, she could climb up the long rope herself and risk falling or being caught in the tree fort with her brother.

What would Tad Walker do? she asked herself.

Unfortunately, she had stopped reading before she learned what Tad Walker decided to do when faced with his two difficult choices. Although there were no poison arrows aimed at her, Bobby McPherson did own a bow and he wasn't afraid to use it! She decided to climb. She didn't want to die alone.

"What happened to you?" Amani said as soon as she entered the tree fort.

It was a mess. Junk everywhere.

"Why are you here?" Hude asked.

"You were taking so long. I didn't know what to do," she said.

"I was looking for the backpack. I couldn't find it, but I did find this."

Hude held up a wrapper.

"Hey, that's my Crickety Crunch. You can't get Crickety Crunch in Maryland."

"You mean it *was* your Crickety Crunch. They ate it."

"Which means that they have been inside my backpack," Amani said.

"Exactly," Hude agreed.

"Hey, Bobby, what do you want to do with this rope. We could tie it up again and make another swing."

"They're here!" Hude and Amani said at the same time, and then shushed themselves.

"Okay. Okay. We need to have a plan. A plan in case they climb up here," Hude said in a hushed and slightly frantic tone.

"We could always jump out the back," Amani said.

Hude peeked out of a space between the boards in the tree fort wall.

"No, we can't do that. It's too high."

"Silly, I was just kidding," she said.

"Well, do you have any serious ideas? We could use one," Hude said.

"I left my brother's slingshot in the fort," Bobby said. "You know how he gets. It'll only take a minute".

Hude and Amani stared straight into each other's eyes. Both knew what that meant. A few seconds later they could feel Bobby right beneath them. The whole fort shook when he started to climb.

"Bobby, come home now! The dog is tearing up the yard again. You need to fill in the holes before Mom gets back. If you're not in the backyard by the time I get there, I swear I'll shoot that dog for target practice. What are you two losers looking at?"

Hude and Amani looked out of the tree fort. It was the same older boy who had been at the archery range at the fairgrounds. Bobby jumped down from the rope. Bobby's friends didn't say a word.

"Are you guys coming?" Bobby said to his friends.

"To your house?" said the boy who had thrown the stone at Amani two days before.

"Yeah, to my house," Bobby said.

"Not with your brother in that mood. Meet us at my house when you're done dealing with the dog. We're leaving now too."

Bobby and his friends walked away.

"Okay, let's go," Hude said. "You know what we have to do, don't you?"

"I know," Amani agreed. "We have to follow Bobby home to see if the backpack is there. Bobby's brother doesn't sound nice at all."

"No, he doesn't," Hude agreed.

Amani climbed down the rope first. She had forgotten to be scared. They followed Bobby on the only other path leading to the lake, until they spotted him. They stayed out of sight as he crossed the street and headed down the sidewalk. He stopped at the corner house and walked around to the back. The backyard was surrounded by a tall, but falling apart, gray wooden fence. Hude and Amani found a part of the fence that allowed them to see inside but still kept them hidden. As they quietly approached, they heard a dog whining. It was a familiar whine. It was Pal.

"Look what they've done to him!" Amani said. "We have to save him too."

Pal was tied up on a short chain. He lay on the ground whining.

Amani looked around. No sign of her backpack. Suddenly, Amani let out a loud gasp. She instinctively covered her mouth.

"What is it?" Hude whispered.

"Mr. Panda!"

Amani pointed to a target hanging on the fence. Mr. Panda was pinned right in the center. One arm was hanging on by a thread, its stuffing exposed. An arrow was stuck in the panda's shoulder and another one in a leg. Its head hung over and fell to the side.

"Incoming!" J.J. McPherson yelled.

An arrow whizzed by. It struck Mr. Panda's head, pinning it against the target.

"Give 10 points to the champion," J.J. McPherson shouted.

J.J. had the same buzzed haircut as Bobby. He was tall and muscular for thirteen. He wore a black T-shirt with a picture of a funny looking skeleton on it, and faded blue jeans that hung low on his hips. He smiled, but his smile did not bring joy.

"And now for the final and fatal shot," J.J. said.

J. J. picked up an arrow from the ground, strung his bow, pulled his arm back, and just as he let go, Pal let out a loud, pitiful whine. The arrow veered off to the left, completely missing the target.

"Shut that dog up, Bobby! Look what he made me do."

J.J. picked up a ball on the ground near him and threw it at Pal. The ball hit Pal on his side and the dog slinked away to another spot. Amani felt sick to her stomach. Pal didn't stop whining.

"We need a plan and quick!" Hude said, "Think, Hude. Think."

"I only see Bobby and J.J. in there," Amani said in a surprisingly calm tone. "I can get their attention somehow and you can jump over the fence, untie Pal, and escape through that hole in the fence on the other side of the yard. We can meet at the lake and run home together."

"I guess you could ring the doorbell until someone answered it. But they probably wouldn't both come," Hude said.

Amani thought for a few seconds. "What if I threw a rock through a front window? That should get them both there."

"I don't know. That's pretty drastic," Hude said.

"We can pay for the window later," Amani suggested. "The most important thing now is to save Pal."

"Wait a second," Hude said. "Do we have to save Pal now? Why don't we run home and get

Mr. Carr. He'll save Pal and take care of J.J. at the same time."

"I guess you're right. It won't take that long," Amani said.

"I'll give you something to whine about!" J.J. yelled.

Bang!

Hude and Amani looked back through the fence. J.J. reached in his pocket and pulled something out. He reached in his other pocket and pulled out a lighter.

Bang!

Pal jumped back. He tried to hide but there was nowhere to go. J.J. pulled out another firecracker, lit it and tossed it even closer to Pal.

Bang!

Pal started frantically pulling on his chain and running around trying to escape. J.J. laughed.

"Stop it, J.J.!" Bobby yelled. "You're scaring the dog."

"It's just a little fun," J.J. said. "Here, let me show you."

J.J. pulled out another firecracker and held the flame of the lighter close to the fuse.

"Don't do it, J.J. Remember what Mom told you," Bobby said.

"But Mom's not here," J.J. smiled.

He lit another firecracker and tossed it near his brother.

Bang!

"Stop it, J.J."

"Come on, it's fun. Here's another."

Bobby didn't wait for the next one to come. He took off through the hole in the fence.

"You can't outrun me, Bobby," J.J. yelled. "I'm better than you at everything. Wait till I catch you."

J.J. chased after his brother. The backyard was now empty.

"This is our chance, Amani. Meet me around the other side, at the hole."

Hude jumped up and climbed over the fence. Pal started wagging his tail furiously when he saw him.

"Good boy. Good boy. Everything is okay now."

Hude patted Pal's back and he whined more loudly than before. But it was a different kind of whine. It was a happy whine. The collar was tight around Pal's neck. It took Hude several seconds to get it off.

"Hurry, Hude. Hurry!" Amani yelled from the other side of the yard.

"Got it! Come on, Pal. We're going home!"

Hude sprinted toward Amani and Pal

followed. But then Pal unexpectedly turned around and went the other way.

"What are you doing, boy?" Hude yelled. "We have to go!"

Pal headed straight for a large trash can in the corner of the yard. He pushed it over and dug through it with his snout. A few moments later he emerged with Amani's backpack in his mouth!

Hude, Amani and Pal didn't stop running until they reached Grandma Hana's yard. They were tired, thirsty, and a little worse for wear, but most of all they were just happy to be home.

"I'll get us some water and then we'll take Pal to Mr. Carr," Hude said.

Pal walked over to Amani and she petted him for the first time.

Hude took out two glasses and a plastic container from the cupboard in the kitchen. He dumped some ice in each of them and filled them to the top with water.

"Here's the water," Hude said, trying to balance everything.

Hude put the container of water down on the patio floor for Pal, remembering the *Hadith* about the man who gave a thirsty dog water and was given paradise.

As Pal gratefully gulped down the water, Mr. Carr walked outside onto his back deck.

Pal didn't hesitate. He dashed to Mr. Carr. In his excitement, Pal knocked Mr. Carr over. To Hude and Amani's surprise Mr. Carr didn't get mad. They couldn't hear what he was saying, but he was petting Pal and was clearly glad to see the dog.

"I thought I heard you," Grandma Hana said when she came outside. "I see that Pal's back, alhamdulillah."

"We found him when we went to the lake," Amani said. "He was tied up in the backyard at that boy Bobby's house. You won't believe what his older brother did."

"I want to hear all about it," Grandma Hana said. "Oh, I see you found your backpack as well," she added. "What happened to it?"

"That's another part of the story," Hude jumped in.

"I forgot all about the backpack!" Amani said.

She picked the backpack up from the patio floor. It smelled awful and a sticky, slimy substance covered half of it. She held her breath and looked inside.

"It's empty, Hude!"

"Everything?" he said.

Amani checked again. "Everything but my pen...Oh, I forgot. I need to check one more place."

Amani opened the backpack and put her fingers down the inside pocket.

"It's here!"

Amani took out the recipe, as if it were a famous painting that had been stolen from a museum.

"Alhamdulillah. We are going to need that recipe soon," Grandma Hana said. "Some peaches should be ready to harvest tomorrow or the day after, inshallah.

It would be perfect timing for the County Fair."

"Are you sure there's nothing else in there?" Hude asked.

"Very sure."

Amani turned the backpack inside out and showed it to him.

"Did you lose something important, dear?" Grandma Hana asked.

"A few things," Hude said.

"I lost my book," Amani jumped in. "Now I'll never know whether Tad Walker traveled down the rapids or climbed up the cliff."

"I'll guess you'll just have to enjoy your own adventures for a while," Grandma Hana said. "It seems to me that you have been having a few since you arrived."

"But they haven't been good adventures, Grandma," Amani said. "Mr. Panda was destroyed. My backpack is ruined. Hude lost some really important things. The new neighbor isn't very nice. We have been having trouble with some boys. We were attacked by monster cicadas and pounded by hail. And most importantly, we still haven't saved the peach tree."

"But the story isn't over yet," Grandma Hana said. "There are blessings in everything. There are blessings in being patient during difficult times. There are hidden blessings that you might not see at first but are revealed later. There are blessings that you may never know about until the Day of Judgment. Allah tells us in the Qur'an: *'It may be that you dislike a thing which is good for you and that you like a thing which is bad for you. Allah knows but you do not know.'* Be one of the patient ones, Amani, the *sabireen*, whom Allah loves."

Just then Pal came running up to Amani, tail wagging and with his favorite red toy in his mouth. He dropped the toy at her feet for her to throw it. As she threw it, she realized that yesterday she couldn't stand the dog. And today all she could think about was saving him.

The last harvest

AMANI looked out of her bedroom window. She couldn't see a thing. It was dark. But more importantly, it was Thursday. Peaches still hung on the tree. Time was running out to bake the pies for the County Fair. She got out of bed and walked downstairs to get a drink of water. The kitchen door leading to the patio was ajar. Amani peeked outside. All was quiet—the birds, the bugs, the trees. Even the wind seemed to be sleeping. Grandma Hana was in *sujud*— peaceful and silent like the world around her. A few moments later she sat up in *tashahud*. She gently placed her hands on her thighs, and one finger extended on her right hand moved slowly back and forth. She then made *tasleem*, whispering to conclude her prayer. She stayed like that for a while, and then, when the time was right, Grandma Hana folded up her straw prayer mat as if it were made of Persian silk. Each movement made, deliberate and graceful, knowing that her Creator watched. Each movement cherished, as if it were her last.

"Grandma, why are you praying out here?" Amani said when her grandmother stood up.

"Everything in creation praises Allah in its own way. Praying outside makes me feel part of that greater community, a community of worshippers that most people forget. Allah has also made the whole world a place for us to pray. I try to pray in as many different places as possible, because the earth will testify for us or against us on the Day of Judgment. I want many good things reported about me."

"Me too," Amani said.

"Breathe in, Amani. What is the air telling you?" Grandma Hana asked.

Amani walked outside and onto the grass. The scent of ripe peaches perfumed the air.

"Are we harvesting today?" Amani exclaimed.

"Inshallah. We'll check at sunrise."

"What's everybody doing out here?" Hude said, rubbing his eyes. He was still half asleep.

"Getting ready to harvest ... inshallah," Amani said.

After *Fajr*, Amani waited by the kitchen window, eager for the sun to rise.

"Grandma," Amani shouted. "A bird just pecked at a peach!"

"Alhamdulillah," Grandma Hana said. "Perhaps it's time."

Amani and Grandma Hana walked to the peach tree. Several branches were nearly touching the ground, curved like an archer's bow. Hude grabbed the new stool that Mr. Fenby had brought over yesterday. Its legs spread, making it far more stable than the one they had used before.

"Hurry, Hude," Amani said excitedly. "I know the peach I'm going to check first. I've been eyeing it for days."

Hude sat the stool down near Amani and she climbed up the steps. The peach was just within her reach. The background was amber gold without a hint of green. It had a nice red blush. The morning sun almost made it glow. Amani cradled the peach in her hand and gently pressed it with the side of one finger. It was not ready.

"I can't believe it! It doesn't have enough give. I was sure that was going to be the first peach picked this year," Amani said disappointedly.

"Amani, come over here. There are a few that I think you should try."

Grandma Hana pointed to a spot near the top of the tree, where the fruit received more sun.

Amani moved the stool to where Grandma Hana was pointing. She tested a few peaches for give. The side of her finger left the slightest indentation on one.

"This is it!" she announced triumphantly.

Amani carefully pulled the peach straight down to break it off the tree. She climbed down the stool and admired her prize.

"My turn," Hude said.

Hude grabbed the stool and placed it a few feet away. He chose peaches differently from Amani. He always looked for the largest peach at the very top of the tree first. He found one swelling with juice. It looked like it might burst at any moment. He rotated it.

"Bummer!" Hude said when he saw the other side. "A bird bit into it."

"You mean, alhamdulillah," Grandma Hana said. According to our beloved Prophet, peace be upon him: '*There is none amongst the Muslims who plants a tree or sows seeds, and then a bird, or a person or an animal eats from it, but is regarded as a charitable gift for him.*'"

"Is this one of those blessings where you think it is bad, but it is really good?" Amani asked.

"It is," Grandma Hana said.

Hude wasn't listening. He was busy examining fruit hanging from another part of the tree. After several attempts, he found his peach.

"Hude, please bring the stool over here."

Grandma Hana breathed in deeply. The fragrance embraced her like an old friend. She climbed up the stool and gently pushed aside some branches. Behind them was a single peach, beautifully framed against the soft blue sky. She knew it was ripe before she touched it. She gave it the gentlest of taps and it dropped freely from the stem.

"Are we ready?" Amani asked.

"I am," Grandma Hana said, as she stepped off the stool.

"Me, too," Hude said.

Amani turned the peach around in her hands, searching for the best spot to bite. She said *"Bismillah"* and opened her mouth widely, sinking her teeth into the yellow flesh. Nectar exploded in her mouth and juice oozed down her chin. It was sweet and tangy. There is nothing like biting into a ripe peach just picked from the tree.

"Awesome," Hude said between bites.

"Alhamdulillah," Grandma Hana said after her first bite. "Hude, please get the wagon. Amani, would you bring the wooden pales? It's time."

Amani burst with joy like a ripe peach

on a tree. It was as if all of nature had heard Grandma Hana. Birds began to sing. Insects buzzed in the air. Leaves rustled in the breeze. Petals opened in the morning light. Everything, it seemed, was celebrating the harvest.

A dark green pickup truck with yellow wording on its side pulled up in front of Grandma Hana's house on Sycamore Street. Fenby Moore and his wife walked around the house to the backyard.

"I knew it!" Mr. Fenby shouted from the patio. "We could smell those peaches ten miles away. So we're gonna have peach pie at the County Fair, after all. What is that word you say, Hana?"

"Alhamdulillah," she called back to him.

"Al...al...alhamdu...Al...hamdulillah, indeed!" Mr. Fenby said.

Amani giggled hearing Mr. Fenby speaking Arabic, and loudly at that.

"Wow! Look at that branch, Fenby. It's so close to the ground," Miss Hazel said as they approached the tree. "I'm surprised that branch hasn't broken off with all that fruit."

"That branch is humble like a knowledgeable scholar, who knows that he doesn't know much," Grandma Hana said. "It's the branches with a few fruit on them you have to worry about. They are mighty and proud, high in the air, thinking that they know a lot."

"Ain't that the truth, Hana," Mr. Fenby laughed.

A car drove past the house, noticing Mr. Fenby's truck parked in front. The driver immediately backed up, jumped out and hurried to the backyard. "Have you started picking?" she asked excitedly.

"We have, Mrs. Ryan," Amani answered with a big smile.

"I'll be back in a jiffy," she said. "I'm going to get Tom and the kids."

Soon neighbors arrived from all directions. They carried lemonade and sweet tea and home-made muffins and pastries to share. People came from all over Cherry Hill. Several families who lived near the *masjid* arrived, even though they lived more than an half hour away. The street was blocked with cars. Everyone was laughing and children were playing. The harvest was here.

"Hude, please ask Mr. Carr if he would like to join us," Grandma Hana said. "Peaches are a gift from God and gifts from God should be shared."

Hude walked to the front of Mr. Carr's house. He didn't see the SUV. He knocked on the door. No one answered. No dog barked. As he walked back, it occurred to him it wasn't losing his video game that bothered him so much. It was losing Grandpop's archery notebook. Seeing his grandfather's handwriting and reading his thoughts had made it feel like his grandfather was still around. And Hude needed him now. He hadn't told Amani, but he didn't think he could beat either Bobby or J.J. McPherson at the archery competition.

"There you are, Hude," Mr. Fenby said. "I've been looking everywhere for you. I have something I want to show you. Let's go inside for a spell."

Mr. Fenby pulled out an old newspaper article. It was yellowish-brown like the pie recipe. The title on the top read 'Local boy wins State Championship!' in big letters. "That is Grandpop!" Hude exclaimed. "Where did you get it?"

"I found it in a box in the basement. I keep old things like this around. I like looking at them from time to time."

The photograph showed a teenage boy in a white tunic, proudly holding a trophy. A strung bow hung on his right shoulder. Over his tunic, a thick leather belt with brass hooks rested loosely on his hips. On his left side, an empty leather bow case hung from the belt connected by two leather straps, so it fell diagonally and toward the front. Hanging from the belt on the right side was a leather quiver full of arrows, fletchings up. It fell diagonally and toward the back. The boy stared straight at the camera. He wasn't smiling but he was content.

"How old was Grandpop here?"

"I believe he was about seventeen years old when he won, not too much older than you. And quite a win it was. It wasn't decided until the last arrow was shot. I didn't notice it before, but you look an awful lot like your grandfather."

Hude studied the photograph for a moment and handed it back to Mr. Fenby.

"Thanks, Mr. Fenby."

"Oh, no. It's yours son. Keep it for inspiration on Saturday. Now, I'm getting myself another peach. I think this is the best year yet."

Hude sat down at the kitchen table and stared at the photograph for a long time.

A few hours later everyone had left. Hude was on the front porch working on his arrow with the suction cup. He figured out that part of his problem was the thickness of the shaft. A thinner shaft shot over more than twenty-five meters catches less crosswind. The arrow flies somewhat faster and has a flatter trajectory, all of which improve long-range accuracy. Instead of using an aluminum alloy for the shaft, he switched it to a smaller diameter carbon shaft that he found in his grandfather's workshop. The arrow still wasn't as accurate as he would have liked, but he had an idea.

Amani was in the kitchen getting organized for cooking pies. Her youthful voice could be heard singing through the open kitchen window. Grandma Hana stared at the peach tree, admiring it in all of its glory. She held a small brown paper bag in her hand. Inside it was a pit. The pit of the first peach picked this summer. A pit from the last harvest.

A lone tear traveled slowly down the side of her face.

Morning jitters

"**A**LHAMDULILLAH, I found it in the attic, Amani," Grandma said, placing a large cardboard box on the floor near the kitchen table.

"He's going to be surprised," Amani said, cutting into a waffle smothered in peach syrup.

"I think so, too," Grandma Hana agreed. "Where is Hude, anyway?"

"He's outside practicing," Amani said.

"*Mashallah*, he is dedicated. Just like Grandpop. And as for you young lady, how do our pies look?"

"Delicious I can't wait to bite into one."

"You know the house rule," Grandma Hana said.

"I know. Judges get the first bite," Amani replied. "Grandma, do you think that Bobby and J.J. will bother us today?"

"I doubt it. They are probably just as focused on the competition as your brother. But if anyone gives you any trouble, you find me. Okay?"

"They are the meanest boys that I have ever met," said Amani. "Although Bobby did try to save Pal from the firecrackers."

"Sometimes people will surprise you, Amani. Only Allah knows what is in someone's heart. At the time of the Prophet, peace be upon him, there was a man named Abu Dharr. His tribe was known throughout Arabia for raiding the caravans that were heading north to Syria. He heard the Prophet, peace be upon him, speak about Islam and converted on the spot. He returned to his tribe and most of them converted through him. He stopped robbing caravans and became one of the Prophet's closest Companions. Probably a lot of people who knew Abu Dharr didn't expect that to happen."

"Grandma, are you still going to talk with Bobby and J.J's mom about what they did to Pal and stealing our things?" Amani asked.

"Yes, but not today. Today, we are simply going to enjoy the Fair and put everything else out of our minds."

Hude walked in the door, sat at the table, and sighed.

"There's this one thing that I just can't get right."

"Well, maybe there's something in here that will help you," Grandma said as she picked up the box and put it on the table. "This is your Grandpop's archery gear."

Hude reached in and pulled out a leather quiver, leather bow case, and a long belt with brass metal hooks on it. There was an Arabic inscription on the front and the leather was carved with a traditional tulip and rose Ottoman design. Without saying a thing, Hude ran upstairs. He returned with the newspaper clipping and laid it on the table.

"These are the same ones that Grandpop used in the State Championship!"

Grandma Hana smiled as she picked up the newspaper clipping. She hadn't seen that photo in years.

"They're replicas from the Ottoman period," Grandma Hana said. "They were designed for horseback riding. The archer would reach down with his right hand and get an arrow out of the quiver on the right side, and pull the strung bow out of the case on the left side. They had amazing aim. Grandpop liked to use them at tournaments. It made him feel connected to the archers of the past. When he shot, he put the belt on the ground. Turkey has a long history of archery, and many of the world's greatest archers have been Turkish. That's why your Grandpop went to Turkey. He wanted to train for the Olympics in Istanbul. There was talk that archery was going to be allowed back in the games. Archery hadn't been in the Olympics for over fifty years because different countries had so many different sets of rules. We met in Okmeydani, a neighborhood that was the center of archery in Turkey at one time. The name means 'arrow-place'. I was there looking at the archery stone columns that have been there for centuries and recorded distances. You might say that archery brought your Grandpop and me together."

"Why were you looking at archery stones, Grandma?" Amani asked.

"I was studying architecture. Istanbul is famous for that. I wanted to build something beautiful, that the whole world would enjoy."

"Did you build something beautiful, Grandma?" Amani said.

"Not what I thought I would build. Grandpop and I got married and we left Turkey shortly after that. He never made it to the Olympics either. But we did make it to 494 Sycamore Street in Cherry Hill in Fairfax County, Maryland. And that was enough for us."

Knock, knock, knock.

A neighbor across the street was at the back door. Grandma Hana motioned her to come in, but only her head came through the door.

"Hana, I was wondering if you would look at something in my garden. It will only take a minute. Mmm, mmm smells like pie to me. See you later at the Fair, kids."

"You both better start getting ready," Grandma Hana said as she was walking out of the door. "We should be leaving soon, inshallah."

"Quick, Amani. We have to talk about the plan," Hude said as soon as they were alone. "When do you think we should start sitting in the tree? I was thinking we start after *Fajr* tomorrow."

"That sounds good to me," Amani said. "I'll take the first shift. I want to spend the morning outside."

"Which brings up the next point," Hude said. "How long should each shift be?"

"I was thinking a few hours," Amani said. "I don't think we have to stay in the tree at night, do you? Nobody is going to cut it down in the dark."

"I agree."

"What about communicating with each other?" Amani asked. "Did you fix the problem with the arrow?"

"Not entirely," Hude said. "Accuracy is still a problem. But I think it may be the fletching so I changed that."

"Hude, I'm really nervous about tomorrow. What if Grandma won't let us stay in the tree? We haven't told her our plan yet."

"Hopefully, it will only be a day or two. I'm nervous about tomorrow as well," Hude confessed. "What if the whole plan doesn't work? What if Mr. Carr doesn't care if the peach tree is declared a treasure of Fairfax County?"

"I'm also nervous about today," Amani said. "Grandma has never lost a pie contest when she baked alone. What if she loses because of me?"

"I'm sure it will be okay. If it makes you feel any better, I'm really nervous about today too," Hude said.

"Do you think you can beat Bobby and J.J.?" Amani asked.

"I don't know. It's going to be tough."

Fenby Moore and his wife pulled up in his truck as Grandma Hana was crossing the street to come back home.

"If you're here for the pie, you are just going to have to wait like the rest of us," Grandma Hana said jokingly.

Fenby Moore didn't say anything. He had a serious expression on his face. Clearly he was there for something else.

"I have bad news Hana and there's no easy way to break it. So I'm just gonna to tell it you straight. Mr. Carr is planning to bulldoze the peach tree today while everyone is at the Fair."

Hana's entire expression changed.

"While we're at the Fair? Why would he do that?"

"I don't know," Mr. Fenby said. "But I suspect he doesn't want a lot of fuss. He knows the whole town will be at the Fair. He's gone and hired someone all the way from Gambrills to come."

"Did you say, bulldoze?" Grandma Hana asked after the words had sunk in. "That doesn't seem necessary."

"I'm really sorry, Hana," Hazel Moore said. "But we thought we should tell you right away."

"And I thank you for that. Whatever you do, please don't tell Amani and Hude. I want them to enjoy today. They have come up with some plan to save the tree, mashallah. I don't know what it is, but I see no harm in keeping their dreams alive for a little bit longer."

"We won't say a thing, Hana," Hazel assured her before they left.

Hana walked to the peach tree for the last time. She picked the peaches that had ripened overnight and even a few that were not yet ready. It stood majestic, a green canopy framed in blue, humble branches laden with glistening fruit. A soft fragrance caressed her, triggering memories of summers past. She reminded herself that if she had never felt sorrow, she would have never known joy.

"Goodbye, old friend. There is so much more I would like to learn from you."

Grandma Hana turned and walked away.

Alhamdulillah,alhamdulillah,alhamdulillah.

The competition

GRANDMA Hana, Hude and Amani sat in the car, waiting to park in a large field next to the fairgrounds. They had been sitting in line for nearly twenty minutes.

"In all my years, I have never had to wait to park for the Fair," Grandma Hana commented.

"Maybe something special is going on, Grandma," said Amani.

"There is. We're together," she said.

A half hour later they were inside the fairgrounds, the very noisy fairgrounds. Every person and every thing seemed to be moving. Brightly colored horses on a mythical carousel rose and fell to the sound of tinkling music. Men with tall top hats and wide striped pants towered over the crowd on hidden stilts. A huge Ferris wheel with red, white, and blue spokes twirled like a giant bicycle against the cloudless sky. Balloons popped. Bells sounded. Sheep bleated. Pigs grunted. Candied apples crunched. Ice cream melted. Children screamed. Babies cried. Old men sat in the shade playing checkers.

Hude noticed none of it. He saw only the fenced field where the competition would take place.

"Grandma, may I go to the archery range to sign in and hopefully do some target practice before the competition?" Hude asked.

"Don't you want to go on some of the rides?" she said.

"Not now. I just need to focus."

"You're just like your Grandpop," Grandma Hana said. "We'll meet you at the target range before the competition starts. We have to register our pies for the contest."

Hude walked toward the archery range. He carried an old canvas duffle bag filled with archery gear. As usual before any tournament, Hude was nervous. Archery is a precision sport. The bow, the arrow, the archer, the environment must all be in perfect sync which each other. A minor change in any one of these could ruin the archer's shot. Each arrow needs to be shot in exactly the same way. The best archers can shoot with their eyes closed. Hude needed to warm up. He needed to shoot some arrows. He needed to feel the shots.

"Grandma, after we drop off our pies I want to ride on those old-fashioned bikes. We tried them a few days ago. They're really fun," Amani said, pointing to a bunch of kids trying to stay balanced on the hi-wheels.

"They look like fun," Grandma said.

"Maybe you can try one," Amani said, smiling.

Grandma laughed. "I may be small, but I think I'm still too big for those. Follow me. We register over here."

Both Grandma Hana and Amani carried a container with a pie in their hands. The contest required each contestant to bake two pies—one for tasting, one for looking at. The contest was held in a large, white tent set up right in the middle of the fairgrounds, so everyone could watch. It was one of the most popular events at the Fair.

Grandma Hana and Amani walked into the tent, passing rows and rows of chairs facing towards the empty stage up front. Rectangular tables were lined up against both sides of the tent. Pies, protected in containers, had been placed in pairs on the first few tables along the left side. In front of each pie was a number. A menacing looking woman sat behind one of the tables guarding the pies. Another woman sat behind a smaller square table on the floor to the left of the stage. Her job was to enter the contestants. As soon as she saw Grandma Hana, she jumped up and tried to hug her, but a pie was in the way.

"It's so good to have you back," the woman said.

"I'm not even going to ask you what kind of pie you're hiding in there. I already know," she said as she sat back down and picked up a pen.

"Wonderful to see you as well," Grandma Hana said. "Amani, do you remember Mrs. Ross?".

Amani did not say anything. She did not remember her.

"Nice to see you again, Amani. You have grown," Mrs. Ross said.

"Please put down my granddaughter's name as well. Amani Habibi. We both baked the pies this year."

"Congratulations!" Mrs. Ross said. "Is this your first contest?"

"Yes," Amani said proudly.

"Well, good luck," Mrs. Ross said. "There is some tough competition this year. Hana, you know Maggie, who lives down on Willow Way. She entered a Key lime pie. We never had one of those in the contest before."

As Mrs. Ross was talking, she wrote on a piece of paper. She handed it to Grandma Hana. It had two names written on it and a number.

"Your entry number is twenty-two. Put your pies on the table next to twenty-one."

"Only twenty-one entries?" Grandma Hana said.

"I think you've scared people away, when they knew you were coming back," Mrs. Ross laughed. "But there's still plenty of time to register. Here comes twenty-three now."

"Oh, fiddlesticks! You caught me," Mrs. Ryan said, holding two covered pies stacked on top of each other.

"What kind of pie do you have, Mary?" Mrs. Ross asked.

"Peach," Mrs. Ryan said sheepishly.

"Why, Mary Ryan," Grandma Hana said jokingly. "Don't tell me you're entering a peach pie with my peaches."

"So, you're not mad at me? Tom thought it was horrible. But I can't go two years again without your peach pie. I thought I would give it a try."

"Mad? Of course not!" Grandma Hana said. "I can't wait to taste what you've done with the peaches."

Amani could not believe what she had just heard. It wasn't cheating, exactly, but it didn't seem exactly fair either.

"Now, this is shaping up to be quite a contest," Mrs. Ross said.

"And here comes twenty-four."

"Amani, let's go if you want to ride those bikes before the archery competition," Grandma Hana said.

Grandma Hana and Amani placed their pies on the table behind number twenty-two. Amani lifted up the top of the container on one of the pies and looked inside.

"It's a beautiful pie, isn't it Grandma?" she said.

The crust was golden brown and flaky. The edges fluted delicately from Amani's slender fingers. In the middle of the pie was the outline of a big peach, hanging from a stem with two leaves. Around the peach was the outline of a heart. It resembled a stick drawing like a child would make, but was made out of dough.

"It is beautiful," Grandma Hana agreed. "I would never have thought of making that design. We make a good team."

"Grandma, would you wait a minute?"

Before Grandma Hana could answer, Amani was already heading back to the square table. She passed Mrs. Ryan on the way who was about to set down her pies. As she spoke to Mrs. Ross, Mrs. Ross pulled out a piece of paper and wrote something down. Amani ran back to Grandma Hana without explaining. Grandma Hana didn't ask.

"Grandma, do you see Hude? I don't see him anywhere," Amani said from the bleachers at the target range about an hour later, after she had ridden the Hi-Wheels Derby ride.

"I don't see him, either" Grandma Hana answered. "But we'll see him shortly. The competition is about to start."

The bleachers were located outside the safety zone and ten feet to the rear of the shooting line. Amani and Grandma Hana sat a few rows up on the bleachers and could see everything easily. They also had a pair of binoculars ready to use, to see where the arrows landed once the competition started. A man holding a microphone walked into the middle of the field.

"Ladies and Gentlemen. We are about to start the Boys Recurve Barebow Individual Competition. The archers will be shooting two rounds of thirty arrows at a 40 centimeter, one spot target face from 18 meters with outer 10 ring scoring. Each round consists of ten ends of three arrows with a two minute time limit. The first round is an elimination round. The top four archers will move on to the final round. The Target Archery Marshal today is Bud Phelps."

Bud Phelps waved to the crowd. He wore a bright red short-sleeved jersey with an insignia on his left sleeve and a camouflage baseball cap. He was easily recognizable.

"We have thirteen competitors this year," the announcer continued. "In order to participate today, they had to qualify by submitting results from previous tournaments. I will call out their names one by one and the archers will line up next to me. John Rawlings, Mark Little, Patrick

Mahoney, Charlie Crawford, Joe Gorman...."

As his name was called, each competitor walked onto the field and faced the spectators. Some smiled. Others looked nervous. None of them said a word. Soon there were only three more archers to introduce.

"J.J. McPherson...," the announcer continued.

"That's him Grandma. That's the boy who tried to hurt Pal," Amani said.

"Yeah!" J.J. shouted, looking at the crowd and putting his fist up in the air. He wore the same short-sleeved black T-shirt with a picture of a skeleton on it. He walked with attitude, as if he wanted to fight.

"Bobby McPherson...."

"That's his brother, the one on the train," Amani said. "Hude has to be next!"

Bobby wore an orange T-shirt with a picture of a racing motorcyclist on it. Unlike his brother, he looked nervous when he walked onto the field and saw all the spectators. He stood in the line next to his brother.

"And our final competitor, Hude Habibi."

Grandma Hana gasped. It was as if she had traveled back in time. Hude was wearing a white tunic over his pants. A strung bow hung on his right shoulder. Over his tunic, a thick leather belt with brass hooks rested loosely on his hips. On his left side, an empty leather bow case hung from the belt connected by two leather straps, so it fell diagonally and towards the front. Hanging from the belt on the right side was a leather quiver full of arrows, fletchings up. It fell diagonally and towards the back. He stared straight ahead. He wasn't smiling but he was content.

The Target Archery Marshal went down the line, inspecting each archer's bow and arrows carefully.

"Archers approach the line!" the Target Archery Marshal said loudly.

The archers took their place on the shooting line. Hude was closest to the bleachers, then Bobby, then J.J, followed by the rest.

"Clear down range!" the Target Archery Marshal yelled to see if the range was clear and safe.

Hude took a deep, long breath and rolled his shoulders to relax. His feet were shoulder-width apart and both feet were even, facing away from the bleachers. His head was nearly perpendicular to his feet, facing the target.

After a few seconds, the Target Archery Marshal said, "The range is clear!" letting the archers know that the range was safe to use.

"Archers may nock and fire three arrows in two minutes for score."

Hude took his stance, nocked the arrow, drew the bow back, aimed and released. The other archers did the same. The range was silent, except for the sound of thirteen large rubber bands snapping.

Thhhip, thhip, thhip....

Thirteen arrows hit their targets. As each archer finished shooting, he lowered his bow, stepped back from the line and waited for the next order.

"Bows down."

The archers put their bows on the ground behind the shooting line.

"Archers may retrieve their arrows!"

All thirteen archers walked anxiously to their target, holding a score sheet. Hude was not happy with his hits. He recorded them as 6, 3, 2. He put one hand on the target face and one hand on the arrow shaft, carefully moving the arrows back and forth to remove them.

All thirteen archers returned to their spot behind the shooting line. The announcer called out the scores to the spectators. J.J. had scored higher than Bobby and Bobby had scored higher than Hude.

"Beat you again. You'll never be better than me at anything," J.J. boasted to his brother. "This is going to be a long day for you."

Bobby ignored him. He was just glad that he was ahead of Hude.

"Archers approach the line!" the Target Archery Marshal said loudly.

Hude took a deep breath, reminding himself that it was only the first three arrows. He had moved his fingers to release, when all he had to do was to stop holding the string. The string itself would push his fingers out of the way. He had also lost focus on the target, thinking about beating Bobby. As his Grandpop always told him, "an arrow cannot hit two targets". Most of all, he reminded himself to relax. In archery, success is found in the archer's relaxation and in the bowstring's tension.

By the seventh end it was clear who the four finalists would be: Joe Gorman, J.J. McPherson, Bobby McPherson, and Hude. When the first round was over, Joe Gorman was in the lead, followed by J.J. McPherson who was 6 points back. Bobby was 13 points back, followed by Hude who was 16 points behind. For most of the first round, J.J. harassed Bobby every chance he got—when they were retrieving arrows, walking back to the line, and, if he could without the Target Archery Marshal hearing him, at the line. Bobby tried to ignore him but it was starting to take a toll on his shooting.

"Grandma Hana," Amani said at the break between rounds, "over there is that kid named Wylie who helped us during the storm. And there's Mr. Carr...," she paused, "...and I think that's Mrs. Carr and his son."

Grandma Hana looked to where Amani was pointing. Mr. Carr was holding a boy of around four years old on his shoulders. A woman was wiping the boy's face with a napkin.

"What are you doing here?" Amani said, looking down.

Pal jumped up on the bleachers to get closer to Amani. She reached down and patted Pal's head. His tail waved rapidly back and forth.

"Pal, come here!" Mr. Carr said.

"Who's that dear?" Mrs. Carr asked.

"Just the neighbors who live behind us," he said.

"Look, they're speaking to one of the archers," Mrs. Carr said as Hude approached Grandma Hana and Amani during the break. "Well, isn't this exciting. We're neighbors with an archer. He seems like a nice boy."

"Pal, come here!" Mr. Carr said again.

Pal ran back to the Carrs. He nearly tackled Mrs. Carr.

"I missed you too, Pal," she said lovingly. "I can't wait to see how the house looks. But what a nice surprise to bring Jimmy to the Fair first."

Mr. Carr had picked up his wife and son at the train station and taken them directly to the Fair. He didn't want them to see the peach tree bulldozed down.

"Ladies and Gentlemen. Please take your seats. We are about to start the second round of the Boys Recurve Barebow Individual Competition. The top four archers who will be competing in the final round are Joe Gorman, J.J. McPherson, Bobby McPherson and Hude Habibi. Archers please line up next to me."

Pal noticed J.J. for the first time. He ran to where Amani was sitting and hid underneath the bleachers near her. He pushed Amani's leg with his nose and started to whimper.

"Don't worry, Pal. He won't hurt you now," Amani said, trying to comfort the dog.

Once again the Target Archery Marshal inspected the archers' bows and arrows before the round began.

"Archers approach the line!" the Target Archery Marshal said loudly.

Not long into the second round it was clear that the leader Joe Gorman was tired. His head started to tilt down and his bow arm started to shake. His draw became increasingly short. By the fourth end he was out with muscle fatigue. Now only J.J., Bobby and Hude remained in the competition.

Hude noticed that J.J. was also getting tired. J.J.'s chest was turning towards the target. He was not as consistent in his shooting anymore. Bobby and Hude were catching up. But Bobby was getting increasingly affected by J.J.'s taunts. Hude watched as J.J would lean over and say something to Bobby when the Target Archery

Marshal wasn't looking. Bobby's face would get red and tighten. At one point J.J. knocked into Bobby as they retrieved arrows. Bobby told him to "stop it!" so loudly that the Target Archery Marshal asked what was going on.

By the ninth end of the second round, J.J was in the lead with 4 more points than Bobby and Hude, who were now tied for second place. Three more arrows would determine the winner.

The Target Archery Marshal called that the range was clear and told the archers to nock and fire. Nine arrows soared through the air. Binoculars could be seen everywhere.

The archers waited for the Target Archery Marshal to give them the command to retrieve their arrows. Hude could not see exactly where his arrows had landed. Some were too close to the lines between the circles, but he knew that he had three good shots.

"Archers may retrieve their arrows!"

The three archers walked quickly to their targets.

"7, 7, 6," Hude wrote down on his score sheet. It was the best end he had scored all day!

Hude looked over at Bobby and J.J. Bobby seemed happy with his score. J.J. did not.

The Target Archery Marshal called out, "Hude Habibi shoots 7, 7, 6. Bobby McPherson shoots 8, 6, 6. J.J. McPherson shoots 5, 7, 4. It's a tie folks!"

The crowd clapped excitedly, Amani most of all.

"According to the rules today, a tie will be broken with sudden death overtime," the announcer began to explain. "Each archer shoots one arrow into their own target and the highest score wins. Archers will be shooting one at a time. If tied again, a second arrow is shot for the highest score. If tied a third time, archers will shoot at the same target and the winner is the arrow closest to the center. The order of the archers will be determined randomly."

Hude shot first, scoring a clean 7. J.J. next, also a 7.

"Don't choke, Bobby boy," J.J. smirked.

Bobby's face tightened as he took his place on the shooting line. He held his bow tightly, pulled his bowstring back and shot. Bobby noticed that when he drew, the bow twisted in his hand. Hude noticed that something didn't seem right with Bobby's form.

The arrow fishtailed, wiggling wildly side to side before hitting the target. The arrow landed somewhere between the 7 ring and 8 ring. If it landed in the 8 ring or on the line between the two rings, Bobby would score 8 and win. There was silence as the Target Archery Marshal checked the target.

"That's a 7!" the Target Archery Marshal shouted.

"Another tie!" shouted the announcer.

The crowd cheered with excitement. The Target Archery Marshal gave the archers the command to retrieve their arrows.

"Don't even think about winning," J.J. told Bobby as they were pulling out their arrows. "You'll be sorry if you even come close to beating me."

J.J. spoke loud enough so Hude could hear what he said.

"Archers, there will be no talking," the Target Archery Marshal warned them.

Hude again went first for the second tiebreaker. He drew and shot.

"That's a 6," called the Target Archery Marshal.

It did not look good for Hude. Both Bobby and J.J. had scored 7s during the day and several 8s. Amani put her hands over her eyes and peeked through her fingers.

"Another 6," the Target Archery Marshal said after J.J. shot.

"Uhh," J.J. grunted loudly, appearing as if he might throw his bow on the ground.

Hude noticed again that J.J.'s chest was turned too much toward the target when he shot. Just as Bobby was taking his stance to shoot, J.J. whispered something to him. Hude could not hear what J.J. said, but he knew he had said something to upset Bobby. Bobby held on tightly to the handle of his bow. Again, the arrow fishtailed wildly in the air before landing.

"That's another 6," the Target Archery Marshal said.

"We have a third tie folks!" yelled the announcer.

As they went to retrieve their arrows, J.J. warned Bobby. "You better miss the target completely this time or else."

That's enough, Hude thought. "Bobby," Hude whispered. "You're holding the riser too tightly. That's why you're fishtailing so much."

Bobby looked at Hude with a puzzled expression. Why would Hude give him advice now? Bobby thought about what Hude had said and recalled that the bow was twisting in his hand after he shot.

"Wait!" the Target Archery Marshal said loudly.

The Target Archery Marshal spoke to the announcer and then approached Bobby.

"Did any of the archers speak to you before you shot," he asked Bobby.

J.J. glared at Bobby. Bobby looked at his brother and shook his head.

"The next person who talks is getting disqualified," the Target Archery Marshal said sternly before nodding to the announcer.

"Okay, folks," we are ready for the final three shots of the day. The arrow closest to the center of the target wins."

The used targets were removed and one new target was set up for all three archers to shoot at. The archers drew straws to determine the order of shooting—J.J. first, followed by Bobby, followed by Hude.

J.J. felt good. His form felt good. He drew his bow and…

"Hummm, hummm," Pal whined when he saw J.J standing on the line alone.

I recognize that, that whine…that dog!

J.J. put down his bow angrily.

"Will the audience please keep quiet," the announcer said.

"That means you, Pal," said Amani.

When it was silent, J.J. drew his arrow and shot. It was a clean hit right in the middle of the 9 ring.

"That's a 9," called the Target Archery

Marshal.

J.J. gave Bobby an icy stare as the crowd cheered.

It was Bobby's turn to shoot next. He remembered what Hude had told him about his grip, and so he relaxed his hand as he held the riser. He drew and released. The arrow shot straight towards the target.

"Bullseye!" shouted someone in the crowd.

The Target Archery Marshal and the announcer walked to the target face.

"That's a 10! Bullseye!" the Target Archery Marshal yelled. "Just this side of the line."

The crowd stood with excitement. Bobby searched for his mother among the spectators. He was smiling for the first time. J.J. was so angry that he took his bow and threw it on the ground.

Hude had one more opportunity to win, but it wasn't going to be easy. He not only had to hit the inner gold circle for 10 points, be he also had to be closer to the center of the target than Bobby. The highest he had scored all day was 8 points. Amani didn't know if she could watch. She huddled close to Grandma Hana as Hude approached the line to shoot.

Hude breathed in deeply. He put the bowstring between the first and second joints of his right hand, using only enough strength to hold the string in position. With his left hand he gripped the bow, letting his hand relax. He raised his head and sternum straight up, which moved his scapulas straight down, exactly where they should be. He pulled back the bowstring just enough to check his form. His bow hand and drawing fingers were relaxed. His scapulas were down. His stance felt stable and he felt aligned. His head faced the target. Everything felt right. Hude pulled the bowstring back towards his chin, focusing intensely on the target. He kept his right elbow up and in line with the arrow. As he continued to move back in a smooth, constant motion, he relaxed the fingers of his draw hand. The string released all of its power, pushing his fingers aside and propelling the arrow forward. Hude knew it was a good shot. He didn't have to look. He felt it.

Thhhip!

The crowd hesitated. Amani stood up. It was too close to call, even with binoculars. The Target Archery Marshal and the announcer walked to the target. There was silence for several long seconds.

"10!" the Target Archery Marshal shouted.

The crowd waited. Still no one knew who

had won. Hude's arrow had to be closer to the center of the target than Bobby's.

"It's a line cutter. Bobby McPherson wins! He's a hair closer to the center," the Target Archery Marshal called out.

"Yeah!" Bobby jumped in the air.

Bobby's mother clapped proudly from the bleachers. J.J. was nowhere to be seen. Amani sat down, disappointed. Grandma Hana smiled as Hude walked over to Bobby to congratulate him.

"Congratulations," Hude said. "That was a good match."

"Why did you help me?" Bobby asked. "You would have won. I couldn't figure out what was going wrong with my shot."

Hude did not answer immediately.

"I guess I didn't like the way your brother was treating you. I wasn't thinking about winning or losing at the time."

"I don't know another person in the world who would have done that," Bobby said.

Bobby suddenly felt terrible.

"I know where my brother hid your video game and that notebook. I'll get it for you. And I'll give back the book too," Bobby hesitated, "as soon as I'm done reading it, if that's okay?"

"That would be great. It is my grandfather's archery notebook," Hude said. "Amani will be glad to get her book back as well. She's dying to know what Tad Walker decided to do."

Hude realized that after everything that had happened during the week, getting his PSP back didn't seem that important anymore. He also felt badly that he had taken it to the lake in the first place, knowing that his intention was to disobey his parents, even if he may have abided by their words. And although he did not win first place, he felt that he made the right choice under the circumstances. He still won some money for coming in second. He would donate it to the County towards buying the peach tree from Mr. Carr, assuming the plan worked out. Even if the plan failed, Hude no longer was interested in buying more video games. Instead, he would buy Amani a new backpack and a new Mr. Panda.

After the prizes and trophies were awarded, family and friends rushed to congratulate the competitors. Pal playfully barreled toward Hude with Amani close behind.

"Good boy, good boy!" Hude said.

Pal wagged his tail and then nudged up against Bobby, clearly wanting Bobby to pet him too. Amani couldn't believe it. Pal wouldn't have been so happy to see Bobby if Bobby had been mean to him. She thought about what

Grandma Hana said about people surprising you, and about not being able to see what is in someone's heart.

"You know this dog?" Bobby asked Hude.

"He's our neighbor's dog," Hude said.

"I found him a few days ago," Bobby said.

"We know," Amani said.

"How do you know that?" Bobby asked.

Hude and Amani told Bobby all about the day at the lake and how they saw Pal in his backyard, and J.J. chasing him out of the backyard with a firecracker. Bobby told them how he had found the dog in the storm and brought him home. Pretty soon they were talking like friends.

The Target Archery Marshal came over to congratulate Bobby and Hude. Bobby told him how Hude had helped him at the end. Bud Phelps could think of only one other archer who would do something like that.

"I knew you were Garrett's grandson," the Target Archery Marshal said, patting Hude on the back several times. "I'd recognize that equipment anywhere, and you look and act just like him. You know we used to call your grandfather Bullseye Brenner."

"You're related to Bullseye Brenner?" Bobby looked at Hude. "Your grandfather is a hero of mine."

As the Target Archery Marshal congratulated other archers, Bobby and Hude talked about his grandfather. Joe Gorman was admiring his fourth place trophy. Amani was petting Pal, while Mr. Carr looked for his dog somewhere else. J.J. McPherson was on his way home. He was in big trouble. Bobby's mother and Grandma Hana were trying to get through the crowd to see their champions. Almost everybody else was rushing to the big white tent for the annual pie contest to begin.

Pie, anyone?

EVERY chair under the big white tent was occupied. The tables lined up on the sides of the tent were now decorated with red-checkered tablecloths and covered with uncovered pies. Each pie on the tables to the left had a number in front of it. The pies on the tables to the right were unidentified. Plates, forks and napkins were neatly placed on the square table on the floor to the left of the stage. In the center of the stage sat a table covered with a white linen tablecloth. Three chairs were placed behind it. On the table in front of each chair were three empty glasses, numerous forks, a napkin, three score cards and a pencil. A glass pitcher of water was off to one side. Several empty chairs were lined up on the left side of the stage. On the right side was an empty round table in the back and a podium with a microphone near the front. Two large, colorful flower arrangements were placed at the front corners of the stage.

Hanging on the tent wall behind the stage was a banner with big black letters that read 'Fairfax County Fair's Annual Pie Contest'.

Mayor Mathews walked up the four stairs to the stage and stood behind the podium. Dixie stood offstage waiting for instructions. Amani grabbed Grandma Hana's hand. They were sitting near the front with the other contestants.

"Good morning. As always standing room only. As you can see from this here, the pie competition is my favorite event at the Fair."

Mayor Mathews rubbed his hands over his protruding belly. The audience laughed.

"We had nearly forty entries this year." Mayor Mathews looked over at Dixie. "Exactly how many are there, Dixie?"

"Thirty-eight," she said.

"We have thirty-eight entries. I think that's some kind of record. Anyway, over the past hour or so Melonie Sheets, owner of Soups Galore and More in Frederick, and Jason Cleary, food critic at the Deerfield Star, have tasted all of them. Tough work they had to do."

The mayor paused while a few people in the audience laughed.

"They have narrowed it down to five finalists, who will be judged by three outstanding food experts, who are now safely out of the way."

Amani sat at the edge of her seat. Her legs were bouncing up and down. She was a bundle of energy waiting to explode.

"Now this is the way it is going to work. I will name the five finalists. They will stay in their seats. We will then bring out our illustrious judges, who don't know who the finalists are. The judges will be given a piece of each of the finalist's pies. Pies will be scored on three attributes: taste, pie design, and the X-factor— something the judges thought made the pie exceptional. Each contestant baked two pies. The judges will taste from one pie and judge the design from the other. Their scores will be combined and a winner will be announced. And in case you want to know, all those pies on your right will be donated to the volunteer fire stations in the area. Should we begin?" the mayor asked loudly.

"Yes!" several people shouted back.

"Here are the five finalists."

Amani held her breath and squeezed Grandma Hana's hand tighter.

"For her blueberry pie, Reece Samson, number thirty-two."

Several people on the left side clapped.

"For her Key lime pie, Maggie Thomas, number eight."

Again, a few people in the audience responded enthusiastically.

"For her peach pie...."

Amani's heart pounded. She listened for her name, but then stopped. She realized that Mayor Mathews had said "her" and not "their".

"Mary Ryan, number twenty-three."

Amani's heart sank. Her smile faded.

"Grandma, they'll never pick two peach pies," she said quietly. "Especially, peach pies made from peaches from the same tree."

Before Grandma Hana could respond the fourth finalist was announced.

"For her caramel pecan pie, Betty Wilson, number fifteen. "And finally, for her...."

Amani heard the word "her" and it felt as if the wind had been knocked out of her. She and Grandma Hana had lost. Or, rather, she had lost the contest for Grandma. She stared at the floor, ashamed to look up.

"Wait a second, folks. For *their* peach pie, Hana Brenner and Amani Habibi, number twenty-two! Congratulations."

"Did he say twenty-two, Grandma?" Amana asked, not sure if she had heard correctly.

"Oh, wait a second. I made another mistake. I should have said, for their peach pie, Hana Brenner, Amani Habibi, and, this is what it says folks, *Mr. Carr!*"

Amani jumped up and hugged her grandmother. Clapping and cheers could be heard all the way to the back of the tent. Hude looked around for Mr. Carr and his family but they were nowhere to be seen. The whole plan to save the tree could fall apart if Mr. Carr was not there. Amani had told him as they walked from the archery range to the big white tent that she had added Mr. Carr's name to their entry because he owned the peaches. She also thought it would make it more difficult for him to cut down the tree if they won. She also pointed out Mrs. Carr and Jimmy.

"Mr. Fenby, I'm going to find Mr. Carr. Would you hold my bow and arrows?" Hude said.

He was sitting next to Mr. Fenby and his wife in the audience.

"I'd be proud to," Mr. Fenby said. "Hurry back. You don't want to miss the contest."

"I know," Hude said and quickly left.

"Settle down. Settle down," the mayor said. "I'm going to get the judges out here soon. Dixie, while I'm introducing the judges would you cut them a piece of each of the finalists' pies? I'm sure some of the ladies will help you. And Tom, since you're so close over there, will you get the finalists' pies and place them on the round table on the stage? Now I'm trusting you, even though your wife's a finalist. So, don't do anything to sabotage the other pies."

Again a few people laughed in the audience. Mayor Mathews walked off stage and out of the tent.

"This is sooooo exciting, Grandma!"

Amani stood up as Mr. Ryan walked by with the finalists' pies, but she could not see the designs on the other pies.

A few minutes later the mayor returned with the judges. Several people in the audience started whispering.

"Please hold your applause until all three of the judges' names have been called. We have Mei-Lin Foo, food critic for the Baltimore Gazette. Antonio Matteo, owner of D.C.'s Capital Pastries. And our special judge from the Food Network show, *Tootie's Goodies*, Tootie!"

Clapping and cheers filled the room.

"We love you, Tootie!" someone shouted from one of the back rows.

"I've seen her on TV, Grandma," Amani said. "I can't believe she will be tasting our pie."

Grandma Hana smiled at Amani, but she wasn't sharing in her excitement. She was starting to put the plan together, or at least she thought she was. Amani had written down Mr.

Carr's name, thinking that it would make it harder for him to cut the peach tree down. Little did her granddaughter know that their beloved peach tree was likely on the ground already.

The judges took their seats on stage, facing the audience. Five pieces of pie lay in front of each judge.

"You may begin, judges," the mayor said.

The audience watched silently, trying to detect any sign of a decision. Each of the judges took a different approach. Mei-Lin Foo, the food critic, cut into the first piece of pie with her fork. She waved the pie in front of her nose, so close she looked like she might inhale it. She then closed her eyes and put the piece of pie in her mouth. She chewed very slowly. She tasted all five pies in this manner before writing down any of her scores. She changed her scores several times as well. Antonio Matteo, the owner of the pastry shop, picked away at the crust with his fork and inspected the flakes. He always tested the crust first, before tasting it. He then tasted the filling, and then finally took a normal bite. He scored each pie as he went and never changed a score. Both judges, however, sipped water between tasting each of the finalists' pies. Tootie, the TV celebrity, had quite an unorthodox approach. She ripped a chunk off of a piece of pie with her fingers and plopped it into her mouth. Then she did the same with another piece of pie. There appeared to be no order to what pie she would taste next. She ate a piece of blueberry pie, followed by a piece of peach, followed by the caramel pecan pie, another peach, and then the Key lime. At one point, she ate three chunks of blueberry pie in a row and then two of Key lime, while completely ignoring the peach and caramel pecan. Throughout it all, she didn't take one sip of water. No one could understand how she could possibly tell the different pies apart.

After the judges had finished scoring for taste, they stood up and moved over to the round table to judge the designs. Here, too, the judges had different approaches. Mei-Lin Foo stared at each pie for a long time. She would then rotate the pie ever so slightly to get another view and stare at it again. She would often rotate a pie a third and fourth time as well. After that, she placed all the pies in a line to look at them together. Antonio Matteo took his time also. The first thing he would do was hold the pie in his hands and move it up and down, as if he were estimating its weight. He held each pie under a bright light on stage and examined it closely. Once he was done looking at a particular pie, he didn't pick it up again. Tootie, on the other hand, glanced at the tables of pies so quickly you wondered if she had a chance to see each one. She then crouched down so low that her eyes were at the level of the table's edge. She looked at a few of the pies from a side angle, turning only one pie to see the other side. She was back in her seat and writing down scores, before the other judges had even really gotten started. When the other two judges finished, Dixie led them out of the tent. Mayor Mathews walked back on stage.

"Listen up, folks," the mayor said. "The judges are comparing their scores and coming to a decision. While that is happening, the finalists are invited to step up on stage and look at the competition."

Amani was the first person on stage. She didn't even wait for Grandma Hana. But soon she wished that she had never left her seat. She lost all hope of winning when she saw the other pies. The blueberry pie was decorated with a thick, intricate matrix that must have taken hours to complete. The caramel pecan pie had swirls of caramel on top, with half pecans perfectly placed in between. The Key lime was topped with a mound of whipped cream that formed a twisted peak in the center. The edges were decorated with candied lime slices. Mrs. Ryan's pie, the other peach pie, was magnificent. The top was a picture of a tree branch, covered with delicate leaves that were chiseled out of dough. Not just any leaves. Peach leaves. Even the other finalists remarked on its beauty. And there, beside all of these works of art, was the childish sketch of a peach inside a heart.

As the contest proceeded, Hude was frantically trying to find Mr. Carr. He first checked the outside arcade, bumping into people and things along the way. Hude searched everywhere but could not find Mr. Carr.

I have to think. I have to think. Where would I want to go if I were Jimmy's age? Hude searched his brain. "The bumper cars!"

Hude ran to the bumper cars and then to the spinning cups and then to the waterslide, but Mr. Carr and his family were nowhere to be seen. He stopped by the concession stands to catch his breath. He would never find them.

Suddenly he was almost knocked over. He looked around it. It was Pal, wagging his tail quickly back and forth. Hude patted Pal's head.

"Yuck!"

Hude's hand came back sticky. Sticky and pink! Hude knew just where to look. And there he found Mr. Carr, Mrs. Carr and Jimmy. They were sitting at a table near the cotton candy stand. Jimmy was holding a half-eaten, gooey ball of pink cotton candy. It was all over his face and hands, and he had some on his clothes.

"Mr. Carr, Mr. Carr," Hude said, catching his breath. "You are wanted at the big white tent immediately. Your name was called. I can show you where it is."

"That's exciting, isn't it dear?" Mrs. Carr said. "Why don't you go on ahead and I'll catch up with you after I clean Jimmy."

"Wait, a second," said Mr. Carr. "What is this all about?"

"I'd rather let the mayor tell you," Hude said.

"Mayor?" said Mrs. Carr. "Well, that sounds even more exciting. Doesn't it, Bradley? Not everyone gets to speak to the mayor. And you have only been here just over a week."

Mr. Carr didn't move.

"Go, on, honey." Mrs. Carr nudged her husband. "You know how much I love surprises. I'm dying to know what the mayor wants with you."

Mr. Carr looked at his wife and turned to Hude, "Let's go."

"You need to walk faster, Mr. Carr, or we will not get there in time."

"In time for what?" Mr. Carr asked.

Beep, beep. Beep, beep.

A golf cart was speeding through the crowd. The crowd jumped out of the way, not quite sure what the young driver was going to do.

"Wylie," Hude screamed when he recognized the clerk from the store. "We need a ride and quick."

"Jump on in," Wylie said.

Mr. Carr sat in the front passenger seat and Hude in the back.

"How did you get this?" Hude asked.

"My friend works here. He let me borrow it on his break. I think I'm going to try this baby out at the cycle track after this," Wylie said with a mischievous smile. "Where are we going anyway?"

"To the big white tent and fast," Hude answered.

"For the pie contest?" Wylie said.

"Pie contest?" Mr. Carr repeated in an angry tone. "Let me ou...."

Before he could finish his sentence and get out of the cart, Wylie drove off. He drove in and out of the crowd like he was on a racetrack. More than one person yelled at him.

"Look out!" Wylie shouted as he turned a corner nearly on two wheels.

Bobby stood motionless in front of the cart, which came to a sudden stop.

"Hude, what are you doing?" Bobby asked.

"No time to explain now," Hude replied, "Jump in."

Bobby jumped in the back seat with Hude. Wylie pushed the gas pedal to the floor before Mr. Carr could escape.

"Let's be quiet, everyone. The judges have made their decision," Mayor Mathews said as the judges walked on the stage and took their seats. "Would the finalists now join them on stage."

Five adults and one child sat in the chairs on the left of the stage. One chair was empty.

"It seems that we are missing Mr. Carr," the mayor announced. "Mr. Carr are you here? Mr. Carr if you are here please come on stage. Has anyone seen Mr. Carr?"

The mayor waited a few seconds longer.

"We'll just have to start without him."

"Here's Mr. Carr. Mr. Carr is here," Hude said out of breath.

"Just in time, Mr. Carr. We've been waiting for you. Please, come take your seat on stage with the other finalists."

Mr. Carr looked at the tent full of people. He looked at the dozens and dozens of pies on the tables. He looked at the mayor behind the podium. He looked at the empty seat on the stage. He was not pleased.

Hude and Bobby sat down near Mr. Fenby and his wife. Mr. Fenby handed Hude back his bow and his belt with the bow case and quiver.

"Now that everyone is here, the judges are about to announce their decision," the mayor said, as excited as everyone else in the room.

"The fifth place winner is Maggie Thomas for her Key lime pie."

The audience applauded. Maggie walked up to the podium and the mayor handed her an envelope. She sat back down.

"Fourth place winner is Reece Samson for her blueberry pie."

The audience applauded and she too received an envelope.

"Third place prize goes to Betty Wilson for her caramel pecan pie."

The audience applauded a little louder. The mayor handed Betty Wilson an envelope and a small trophy as well.

"Would the remaining finalists please come to the front of the stage," the mayor said.

Mrs. Ryan was standing at the front of the stage first. Grandma Hana and Amani followed. Mr. Carr stood up last. Amani and Grandma Hana held hands. Amani looked at the stage floor. She did not want to see Grandma Hana's face when they lost.

"The winner of this year's pie contest is ..." the mayor paused as he opened the sealed envelope. "The winner is number twenty-two. Hana Brenner, Amani Habibi and Mr. Carr!"

People clapped and cheered. Armani jumped when she was sure their names had been called. She was not expecting to win. Mrs. Ryan's pie was so much prettier. She grabbed onto Grandma Hana. Soon every one on stage was congratulating every one else, except for Mr. Carr. He was trying to sneak away. Dixie caught him on the steps and pushed him back on stage.

"Would every one please take their seat again? Tootie is going to speak for the judges now."

The room was silent. Everybody wanted to hear what the famous chef had to say. Tootie walked up to the podium and smiled directly at Amani.

"All of the pies were delicious and special in their own way. I could not have baked a batch of better pies myself, and I am not just saying that. The blueberry filling was to die for, not too sweet and the right consistency. The Key lime pie was light and fluffy and so refreshing. We appreciated that no food coloring was used. We loved the caramel sauce. We could tell it was home-made. And I'm not leaving this Fair without that recipe. And what more can be said about Mrs. Ryan's peach pie than it was truly a masterpiece. I have never see dough shaped so beautifully. I can only imagine the time it must have taken to do that. There wasn't too much cinnamon and we detected another spice that was delightful, although we disagree on what it is.

"But the winning pie stood out among the rest. We all agreed. The crust was perfect in taste, color and flakiness. And while the designs on all the other pies are wonderful, they ever so slightly distracted from the taste. If a crust is a little too thick or too sweet or adds a new incongruent flavor, the pie becomes two parts— the filling and the crust. But if the crust and the filling are in perfect harmony, inside and out, each contributes its own flavors and textures, but the taste is one.

"And as for the filling, it was unlike anything I have ever tasted before. The peach flavor was pure and fragrant. I don't think any spices were used, except maybe a little salt. Is that right?" Tootie looked at Amani.

Amani nodded her head. "Yes," she said.

"About seven or eight peaches are needed to make a pie. To grow that many peaches that taste so consistently delicious is nearly a miracle. The soil, sun, water, and air would have to be just right and for the entire season. The peaches would have to be picked at exactly the right time and cooked just at their peak. To accomplish this impossible task, these peaches had to have been grown from a tree in someone's backyard. And the tree would have to be spectacular and the bakers bursting with love. And that is the X-factor!"

At first the room was silent and then it erupted. People rose to their feet, clapping and cheering. People were laughing. People were smiling. Mrs. Carr cried, as she and Jimmy made their way to the stage. Amani and Hude rushed to speak with Mr. Carr. Grandma Hana, Mr. Fenby and his wife followed. Mayor Mathews and Dixie were not far behind.

"You see, Mr. Carr, you just can't cut down the peach tree. It's spectacular. You heard it yourself," Amani cried.

Mr. Carr opened his mouth to speak. Before

any words could come out, Dixie shoved a piece of the pie in his mouth. "I'm sure you will change your mind after you taste this."

The mayor unwrapped a plaque and put it right in front of Mr. Carr's face.

"Surely, you are not going to cut down the treasure of Fairfax County."

Everybody was staring at Mr. Carr. Everyone was waiting for an answer.

Mrs. Carr rushed to her husband on stage and said with tears in her eyes, "My grandmother and I used to bake pies together. Some of my best memories are our trips to the orchard. Why didn't you tell me you entered the contest? Why didn't you tell me we had such a spectacular tree in the backyard?"

Mr. Carr was silent. He looked at his watch and pulled out his cell phone and dialed.

"We have to leave, NOW!" Mr. Carr yelled unexpectedly a few seconds later. "The bulldozer is scheduled to take down the tree in less than fifteen minutes and no one's answering the phone!"

They all ran to the entrance of the fairgrounds. By this time, Mr. and Mrs. Ryan, Bobby, Wylie, along with Tootie and the other judges who had been listening on stage, joined them. The Target Archery Marshal was there as well.

"We'll never be able to get there in time on the roads, even if we use the fire engine," the mayor said. "The street looks like a parking lot."

"What about the golf cart?" Wylie said.

"It may be able to get through the cars but it's not fast enough," Mr. Carr said.

Think, Hude, think, he thought to himself.

"Come back here, Jimmy!" Mrs. Carr called as he ran towards the Hi-Wheels Derby ride.

"That's how we'll do it!" Hude exclaimed.

"Of course!" Amani knew exactly what Hude was thinking. "We'll use the cycle track and back paths to get to Sycamore Street!"

Hude and Amani quickly explained their plan to everyone. Together they ran over to the Hi-Wheels Derby ride. The mayor convinced the employee working at the ride to let them borrow some of the hi-wheels. Hude was wearing his belt with the attached bow case and quiver. He pulled out the strung bow with his left hand and hung one side over his right shoulder and the other side under his left arm, string forward. He quickly jumped on one of the hi-wheel bikes. Amani, Bobby and Wylie did the same and they started to ride away.

"Mr. Carr, are you coming?" Amani yelled. "Only you can stop the bulldozer."

"Go, honey, go!" Mrs. Carr screamed.

Mr. Carr picked up a hi-wheel and sat down on the undersized seat. He was clearly too big for it. With his feet precariously on the tiny pedals, he tried to balance himself. His knees extended to his ears in both directions. He looked like a clown riding a miniature bike, only funnier.

"I can't ride this thing. It's much too small," Mr. Carr said.

"Wait!" the operator of the ride shouted.

Thirty seconds later she returned with another hi-wheel.

"It's a little bigger," she said. "Still not full size but it should be better."

Mr. Carr hopped on the bigger hi-wheel. He still looked ridiculous.

"Don't worry about how you look, Mr. Carr," screamed Dixie. "Just RIDE!"

Hude, Amani, Bobby and Wylie headed for the cycle track, with Mr. Carr following behind them. The race to Sycamore Street had begun!

The great race

MR. CARR thought he might die and he hadn't even reached the cycle track yet. While the others on the hi-wheels were maneuvering surprisingly well through the crowds, he was barely able to keep his balance. Every person and every thing seemed to be jumping right in front of him. Kids playing tag on brightly colored stick horses ran in front of him, nearly knocking him over. He swerved to avoid them and headed straight for a man on stilts wearing a tall top hat. At the last moment, the man spread his long legs and Mr. Carr rode right between two walls of wide stripes. Mr. Carr was a menace on wheels. As he passed, balloons popped, bells sounded, sheep bleated, pigs grunted, candied apples dropped, ice cream melted, children screamed, babies cried, and old men sitting in the shade looked up from their checkers. A huge Ferris wheel with red, white, and blue spokes twirled like a giant bicycle wheel against the cloudless sky. But no one seemed to notice. All eyes were on Mr. Carr.

"Come on, Mr. Carr," Amani yelled, as they headed toward the dirt track. "Try to stay on the flat part. And watch out for the curves."

Banks! Curves! Here goes!

Mr. Carr decided that his safest bet was to focus on steering and balancing, and not pedaling. He took his feet off the pedals, rested them on the bike frame, and clutched onto the steering wheel with all his might.

"Whoa, whee, wahoo, oh dear, phew, uh-oh." Mr. Carr rapidly raced down the hill toward the others.

In fact, because Mr. Carr was heavier, he passed the other hi-wheelers near the end of dirt track. But he was not prepared for it to stop so abruptly.

Bing. Bang. Twirl. Plop. "Ouch!"

He did a series of acrobatic maneuvers before landing hard on the unpaved dirt.

Mr. Carr jumped up, brushed himself off and yelled, "Let's go!" as he got back on his hi-wheel.

Soon the other hi-wheelers were ahead of him again. Up ahead stood the yappy dog Amani and Hude had seen last time, barking and blocking the path.

"Get out of the way!" Wylie, who was in the lead, yelled.

The little dog was undeterred, determined to stand its ground.

"It'll move," Wylie called back to Hude who was right behind him.

But he was wrong. The dog did not move. In order to avoid rolling over it, Wylie swerved out of the way. He lost his balance and he and his hi-wheel went tumbling into the adjacent field.

When he stopped, he sat up and picked some grass out of his mouth. Beside him lay a large front wheel that was broken and bent. Wylie was out of the race.

Meanwhile, Hude, who was right behind Wylie, managed to miss the little dog and so did Bobby, who was next. Amani was not so lucky. The dog apparently recognized her and started chasing her, nipping and yapping. The faster Amani pedaled, the faster the dog ran.

Suddenly, Amani felt a bump and heard silence. She looked down. White fluff was spinning around and around in the spokes of her large front wheel. Before she had time to react, the dog spun out of the wheels and flew directly at Mr. Carr who was behind her. Instinctively, Mr. Carr let go of the steering wheel and caught the flying canine. In the process, though, he lost his balance and he and the dog and the bike rolled along the dirt path. When Amani found him, the little dog was in Mr. Carr's arms, licking his face. The hi-wheel was in pieces.

"Come back!" Amani called ahead to Hude and Bobby. "Mr. Carr is down."

Hude and Bobby rode back as fast as they could.

"I'm sorry, kids. I let you down. This is all my fault," said Mr. Carr.

Amani thought for a moment. "I have an idea. What if you wrote a note and we could give it to the bulldozer driver. We could at least stop him until you came." "I can show you the way, Mr. Carr," Wylie said, holding the two parts of his broken hi-wheel.

Amani reached in her back pocket and pulled out a sheet of folded, lined paper and a little pink pen. In big capital letters, she wrote "STOP! PLEASE," followed by a smiley face.

She handed the pen to Mr. Carr, who wrote "I'll be there soon" and signed his name.

"Here, Hude. You take the note. You ride faster than me."

Amani handed the note to Hude. To keep it safe he reached for the arrow with the red suction cup for a tip and plastic Spin Wing vanes for fletching. He quickly tucked the note in the scroll attached to the shaft.

"Let's go!" Hude said when the note was safely tucked away.

The remaining three hi-wheelers in the race rode off. Mr. Carr, who was still holding the little white dog, and Wylie, followed on foot.

Hude, Bobby and Amani came to a screeching stop at the bridge. It had finally crumbled. They looked at the water below them. They didn't know how deep it was or what was in it.

"What would Tad Walker do?" Bobby said to Amani.

Amani looked at Bobby with surprise and smiled.

"The rope swing!" she yelled. "But we'll have to leave the bikes."

Bobby pulled on the tattered rope. It seemed sturdy enough—at least he hoped.

"I'll try it first," he said.

Bobby swung across, easily landing on the other side.

"It's fine," he called back and swung the rope to Hude.

"You go next, Amani," Hude said.

Amani gave it all she had. She started off well but began to slow down as she approached the other side.

"I'm not going to make it!" she screamed.

Bobby reached out and caught the rope. Amani was now safely on the other side.

It was now Hude's turn. He swung easily across, resembling Robin Hood, with a bow across his body and full quiver of arrows hanging from his side.

There was nothing left to do but run. Grandma's House on Sycamore Street was nearly a half a mile away. Bobby, who had years of training from running away from his brother, took the lead. Amani easily kept up. Two times in the past week she had run a much farther distance back from the lake. Hude pulled the bow over his head and gripped the riser with his left hand and squeezed the bowstring to it, resting both his hand and bow against his left shoulder. The empty case and quiver bounced against his body as he ran but he barely noticed.

As they approached 494 Sycamore Street a loud engine and the sound of creaking metal could be heard from the back. Bobby and Amani reached Grandma Hana's house first.

"We're too late!" cried Amani from the side yard.

All they could see was the enormous steel blade of the bulldozer, approaching right behind the peach tree. The blade's sharp cutting edge was in the air, jerking back and forth, making a horrible noise. The driver could not control it. But then the blade stared to move down. Hude realized that there wasn't enough time to get to the bulldozer in time. The bulldozer was at least sixty meters away from Grandma Hana's side yard.

Think, Hude. Think!

With his right hand Hude reached in his quiver and brought the arrow with the new vanes forward, suction cup first. In one fluid motion he nocked the arrow, drew the bow, anchored, aimed and let the string push his fingers out of the way. Hude, Amani and Bobby watched as the arrow ripped through air, passing cleanly through a blue space in the peach tree. The suction cup landed crisply, smack in the middle of the protective shield of the bulldozer's cab. Confused, the driver got out of the cab to see what was stuck on his windshield. He read the message, "STOP! PLEASE. ☺," written on a piece of lined paper in big pink letters.

Hude, Amani and Bobby sprinted to the peach tree to explain. About ten minutes later, Wylie, Mr. Carr and the little white dog showed up.

Waa waa waa waa waa WAA WAA WAA WAA. The loud whine of a siren approaching could be heard barreling down the street. An old red, shiny fire engine turned the corner and screeched to a stop in front of Mr. Carr's house.

The mayor jumped out from the fire engine first, followed by the fire chief, Dixie, Mrs. Carr and Jimmy, who cried because he didn't want to get out. Seconds later, Mr. Fenby pulled up in his pickup truck. Mrs. Moore sat next to him in the front seat and Grandma Hana next to her. Sitting in the long bed in the back were Mr. and Mrs. Ryan, the Target Archery Marshal, a yellow Labrador retriever, a food critic, a restaurant owner and a celebrity.

Endings and beginnings

EVERYONE gathered around the peach tree. Everyone was eating pie. Mr. Fenby sat with his legs outstretched next to his wife. Mayor Mathews and the fire chief stood in the grass nearby, telling stories from the past. Tom Ryan and the bulldozer driver stretched out in the sun, enjoying the cool breeze. Mrs. Ryan, Mrs. Carr and Dixie huddled together, giggling like schoolgirls. Hude leaned against the trunk of the peach tree, explaining to Bobby, Wylie and the Target Archery Marshal how he had constructed the arrow. Tootie and the other judges searched for the perfect peach. Mr. Carr lifted Jimmy high into the tree to smell the ripening fruit. The little white dog lay sleeping between Pal's extended paws, as if they had always been best buddies. A delicate butterfly landed on a ripe peach, unnoticed.

Amani and Grandma Hana sat a slight distance back, watching.

"I was thinking, Grandma," Amani said. "If Bobby had not been on the train, if Mr. Carr had not moved in, if I had never left my backpack at the lake, if the storm had never happened, if Pal had not run away, if the road had not been blocked, if the little dog had not gotten stuck in my spokes, if the bulldozer had not come, none of us would be here right now. So although a lot of things happened that seemed bad at first, it worked out really well in the end."

"Subhanallah," Grandma Hana said.

"I was thinking something else too," Amani continued. "You said that you wanted to build something beautiful. You did build something beautiful. You built a community, a community of love."

It was as if all of nature had heard Amani's words. Birds began to sing. Insects buzzed in the air. Leaves rustled in the breeze. Petals glowed in the afternoon light. Everything, it seemed, was celebrating the end of the great race to Sycamore Street.

Acknowledgments

All praise belongs to Allah alone, and may Allah's
blessings and peace be upon the Prophet Muhammad,
his family and companions. I write books that I want my
children to read—books that are entertaining as well as
instructive. *The Great Race to Sycamore Street* is a fun
adventure story with life lessons scattered throughout.
It teaches the importance of problem solving and acting
with integrity in difficult situations. It reminds the reader
how much there is to learn from nature and that by
working together great things can be accomplished. I
would like to express my gratitude to all of my teachers,
young and old, human and otherwise. *Alhamdulillah*.

References

Islam is based on two primary sources, the Qur'an and *Hadith*. Muslims believe that the Qur'an is the speech of God revealed through the Archangel Gabriel, peace be upon him, to the Prophet Muhammad, blessings and peace be upon him, over a period of 23 years. *Hadith* (capitalized) refers to collections of statements and actions of the Prophet Muhammad, blessings and peace be upon him, as well as what he silently approved in other people's actions. An individual *hadith* (lowercase), among other things, may explain a verse in the Qur'an, teach good character or conduct, or how best to practice Islam. Specific verses in the Qur'an and *ahadith* (plural of *hadith*) are mentioned in *The Great Race to Sycamore Street* because Muslim parents and guardians often refer to these two sources when instructing children on how to behave and what constitutes good character. Thus, it would be unusual for a story involving Muslim characters not to mention the Qur'an or some *ahadith*. The *Hadith* of Gabriel is a particularly important because it sets forth the three dimensions of the Islamic religion, submission to God (Islam), faith (*Iman*) and beautiful conduct (*Ihsan*).

References to the Qur'an

References to ahadith

Numerous sayings and actions of the prophet Muhammad, peace be upon him, were referred to in *The Great Race to Sycamore Street* relating to social and moral virtues. They include feeding God's creatures (p99), being slow to anger and quick to calm (p33), being good to neighbors (pp36–37), following a bad act with a good one (p85) and controlling one's anger (p55). To see the full list of references to ahadith in *The Great Race to Sycamore Street* please visit www.kubepublishing.com, or request it from info@kubepublishing.com.

Due to it's importance, the *Hadith* of Gabriel, referred to on P37, is quoted in full below.

'Umar ibn al-Khattab said:
As we sat one day with the Messenger of Allah (Allah bless him and give him peace), a man in pure white clothing and jet black hair came to us, without a trace of travelling upon him, though none of us knew him.

He sat down before the Prophet (Allah bless him and give him peace) bracing his knees against his, resting his hands on his legs, and said: "Muhammad, tell me about Islam." The Messenger of Allah (Allah bless him and give him peace) said: "Islam is to testify that there is no god but

Allah and that Muhammad is the Messenger of Allah, and to perform the prayer, give *zakat*, fast in Ramadan, and perform the pilgrimage to the House if you can find a way."

He said: "You have spoken the truth," and we were surprised that he should ask and then confirm the answer. Then he said: "Tell me about true faith (*iman*)," and the Prophet (Allah bless him and give him peace) answered: "It is to believe in Allah, His angels, His inspired Books, His messengers, the Last Day, and in destiny, its good and evil." "You have spoken the truth," he said, "Now tell me about the perfection of faith (*ihsan*)," and the Prophet (Allah bless him and give him peace) answered: "It is to worship Allah as if you see Him, and if you see Him not, He nevertheless sees you."

He said: "Now tell me about the Hour." The Prophet (Allah bless him and give him peace) answered: "The one who is asked about it knows no more than the questioner."

He said: "Then tell me about its signs." The Prophet (Allah bless him and give him peace) answered: "That a slave girl shall give birth to her mistress, and that you see barefoot, naked, destitute shepherds vying to build tall buildings."

Then the visitor left. I waited a long while, and the Prophet (Allah bless him and give him peace) said to me, "Do you know, 'Umar, who was the questioner?" and I replied, "Allah and His messenger know best."

He said, "It was Gabriel, who came to you to teach you your religion"
(Sahih Muslim)

Glossary of Islamic terms

Alhamdulillah: Praise belongs to Allah

Allah: The proper name of God

Astaghfirullah: I ask Allah's forgiveness

Baba: Loving name for father

Fajr: Dawn prayer

Haram: Forbidden in Islam

Hadith: Reports (verbal or written) of statements and actions of the Prophet, Allah's blessings and peace be upon him, as well as what he silently approved in other people's actions

Iman: Faith

Inshallah: If Allah wills

Jannah: Paradise

Mashallah: What Allah wishes

Masjid: A place of prostration; mosque

Qur'an: Holy book of Muslims

Shahadah: Testimony of faith; what someone says to convert; one of the five pillars of Islam

Subhanallah: Glory to Allah

Sujud: Position during the Islamic prayer where the person prostrates and their face hands, knees, feet are on the ground

Sunnah: Practices and beliefs of the Prophet Muhammad, blessings and peace be upon him, that Muslims strive to follow

Tashahhud: Statement made during formal prayer that includes the *shahadah*

Tasleem: Statement, *"As salamu 'alaykum"* ("Peace be upon you"), which terminates the formal prayer

Zakah: Obligatory charity given on annual basis; one of the five pillars of Islam

Glossary of archery terms

Anchor point: The fixed position of the bowstring hand on the jaw or cheek while holding or aiming

Arm guard: A protective strap to protect an archer's forearm when shooting

Arrow rest: A device attached to the bow to set the arrow upon instead of the hand

Barebow: A bow that does not have attached to it mechanical stabilizers or sights or other "high tech" gadgets

Bullseye: The center of the target where the archer scores the most points

Chest guard: A protective strap to protect an archer's chest when shooting

Draw: When the archer pulls back the bowstring into the shooting position

Draw check indicator: A device used to inform the archer how far back to draw the bow

End: A group of arrows (typically 3, 5, or 6) shot together before going to the target to score and retrieve them

Field archery: Shooting at targets at varying distances in an open field, rough or wooden terrain

Finger tab: A small leather patch to protect the archer's three drawing fingers from blistering

Fletching: Feathers or plastic attached to the end of the shaft to stabilize the arrow in flight and improve accuracy

Kisser button: A button placed on the bowstring that touches the archer's lip when the bow is drawn, allowing the archer to maintain consistency in shooting

Nock: The notch in the end of an arrow that holds the arrow in place on the bowstring; as a verb nock or nocking means to place the arrow on the bowstring

Nocking point: The point on the bowstring where the arrow is placed before the archer draws and shoots the arrow

Quiver: A container for an archer's arrows

Recurve bow: A bow where the tips curve away from the archer when strung

Riser: The areas of the bow just above and below the grip

Shaft: The long, straight part of the arrow where other parts are attached

Sight: A device placed on the bow or string that an archer uses to help in aiming at the target

Stabilizer: Weight attached to the bow to give it balance and absorb shock

Target archery: Shooting at non-moving targets from set distances

Tip: The front end of the arrow

Vane: A term often used to describe fletching made of plastic or rubber instead of feathers